CODA

AMERICAN POLITICS, PERSONAL LOSS, AND RECOVERY

A NOVEL

DICK BISHIRJIAN

En Route Books and Media, LLC
St. Louis, MO

ENROUTE
Make the time

En Route Books and Media, LLC
5705 Rhodes Avenue
St. Louis, MO 63109

Cover design by Avery Easter

LCCN: 2020943809
ISBN-13: 978-1-952464-25-6

Dedicated to David Katz

Founder, Coda Gallery
Palm Desert, California

Contents

Prologue

Mary Hill was happy living in Allentown in Eastern Pennsylvania—about 60 miles from Philadelphia—but she also knew that her place was with Bob.

Mary Hill flew into Reagan National where Chris Murphy picked her up and brought her to Congressman Hill's House Chambers in Cannon, House Office Building, or "HOB," as Congressional buildings for House members are called.

Named for "Uncle" Joe Cannon, Speaker of the House from 1903-1911, a Republican from Illinois, who controlled every piece of legislation of his day, Cannon House Office Bldg. (HOB) was the first of the House office buildings and was built for the ages. Each office had a small foyer with two reception desks, an office for the House member and another for staff. In-between was a small space for meetings with groups of visitors. At most, ten people could squeeze into that space.

Chris Murphy was a typical "staffer," bookish look-ing, shorter than his "Member," Bob Hill, and visibly

1

showing his concern to do well for his boss. That meant wearing a Hart Schaffner and Marx suit, and blue shirts with ties that matched. His suits looked expensive, but he bought them at an annual sale that the company held for policemen, firemen and their immediate families.

That a company would do that impressed Chris, and he was even more impressed when he learned that Mr. Marx had emigrated from Communist Russia and donated a large sum to the University of Chicago in support of one of Chicago's best free market economists.

Life was good for Chris Murphy and got better when, after two terms, his boss was elected to the U.S. Senate.

Mary had helped interview the two receptionists, nice girls from a local clerical school, and interviewed the person chosen to be the Congressman's Chief of Staff.

Mary liked Chris Murphy from the first day that she met him and encouraged Bob to hire Chris and leave the other hires to Chris.

In the old days, the Postmaster General was the chairman of the President's Party, and Members on the Post Office subcommittee used the power of their position to direct where U. S. Post Offices would be built and make Postmaster appointments to reward constituents.

In the 1960s, that type of patronage was superseded by defense contracts, and the District of Columbia was built out and the scent of money was in the air. At stake were contracts for tens of millions of dollars for weapons systems, and major and minor defense contracts were outsourced by reference to defense needs and politics. If you follow how defense contracts are awarded, you will understand who has power in the United States.

But Bob Hill fought for assignment to the House Foreign Affairs Committee—a plum not usually given to Freshmen and reserved for Members whose Districts were secure. Spending time on foreign affairs had its downside since constituents wondered when their Congressman would pay attention to their issues. If a member's district became marginal, appointment for Foreign Affairs could become a terminal appointment. But, Bob Hill knew that knowledge of foreign countries and the balance of power among nations was a weakness of most Americans, including himself, and he saw Foreign Affairs as the best way to learn. After all, he would need that knowledge when he was President.

Bob Hill's reading about the history of Presidential Administrations taught him that, with the exception of Dwight Eisenhower, Richard Nixon and George H. W. Bush, most Presidents from 1960 through the present day were ignorant of political currents two feet off the East or West coasts of the United States. And many of their failures were related to that lack of knowledge.

John F. Kennedy misjudged Fidel Castro and the Soviet Union, allowing Castro to stay in power when an invasion President Kennedy authorized failed. And the Berlin Wall was built on JFK's watch.

Lyndon Johnson mired the United States in a tragic land war in Asia.

Jimmy Carter might have been re-elected but for his mishandling of the Iran hostage crisis.

Ronald Reagan got tied up in a tussle with Marxists in Nicaragua and Islamic radicals in Teheran that almost brought down his Presidency.

George H. W. Bush was co-opted by the People's Republic of China when he was Ambassador to the PRC and continued to play Richard Nixon's "China card" long after there was a card in the game to be played between the PRC and the Soviet Union. On June 4, 1989, when freedom demonstrators at Tiananmen Square were mowed down by troops with assault rifles,

President George H. W. Bush failed to act.

Another limb from the same bush, George W. Bush—easily one of the most foolish of all Presidents—except for Jimmy Carter—made the mistake of allowing his personal feelings to expand his Administration's invasion of Afghanistan into invasion of Iraq. Consumed by the immense power of the Presidency and motivated by religious beliefs of a large group of his supporters, "W" sought to hasten the Second Coming of Christ by bringing democracy to the Middle East.

Bob Hill was familiar with that history and the foreign policy failure of American intervention in the war in Bosnia and Herzegovina of Bill Clinton.

But, the young Congressman couldn't explain why American voters elected Barack Obama to the office of President—not once, but twice—when it was clear his sympathies for the Muslim world and training in Lenin's teachings modified American foreign policy toward the Islamist regime in Iran and the Communist regime of Fidel Castro in Cuba.

If he became President, Bob Hill vowed to have the best foreign policy and keep the United States out of another war.

1.

In the Beginning

Chris Murphy, now looking like an important Chief of Staff to an attractive U.S. Senator Bob Hill, was attracting the interest of large banks, investment advisors, and Savings and Loans from Pennsylvania. To keep his sense of reality, he was helping his father close his family's tiny vacation cabin near Keisters Farm in Slippery Rock, Pennsylvania, on September 11, 2001.

The cabin had been built in 1952 off Rte. 8, overlooking Slippery Rock Creek, by his grandfather and father who hollowed out a space big enough to lay a foundation, install one door, two windows and a wall that divided a sleeping area from the kitchen area. The facilities were outside in an Outhouse.

Not much had been done to improve it, but it was a fun place to hold family picnics in summer and around Labor Day.

Chris looked good in suits, but he preferred the frayed jeans that he wore around the cabin.

When he thought of the cabin he'd remember that feeling he got when he knew that on Monday after Labor Day he'd be back in school.

Though his family of first generation Americans of Irish and Welsh descent were Democrats, on 9/11 Chris decided that he was a Republican. That idea had been brewing in his mind since his freshman year at the University of Pittsburgh. At Pitt, he fell in with students from Republican families and gravitated toward them from friendship and his own political leanings.

But his announcing that decision was not taken well by his grandfather and father. His grandfather had experienced hunger during the Great Depression, had attended public high school in Pittsburgh, had enlisted in the Marines in World War II, and had worked in a Pittsburgh steel mill, ultimately becoming a union leader for the United Steel Workers.

His father did not go to college, but became an automobile mechanic while serving in the U.S. Navy in World War II, ultimately owning his own series of gas stations, first in East Liberty and later in Wilkinsburg, a suburb of Pittsburgh. He owned the stations, but the price of gas was controlled by City Service and Gulf, and each station had only one garage for oil changes and minor tune ups.

Life had been hard for both of them, and his father never earned much above what today is designated as the "poverty level."

Chris Murphy's family was white, working class and poor, and it bothered them that their pride and joy, Chris Murphy, was a Republican.

Chris was the first member of his family to go to college and was unprepared from his first college days at the University of Pittsburgh for the Liberal bias of his college teachers. It was hard for him to understand that they didn't share his love for Pittsburgh's many ethnic groups, their religions, and the America that the Pittsburgher's loved.

More than once, Chris heard his grandfather tell him that America is the best country in the world.

He never heard that spoken by Pitt professors.

Working-class Pittsburghers like Chris, his grandfather and father were what Sen. Hill's pollster, Steve Weissman, called "urban ethnics."

James Carville was only partly right when he described Pennsylvania as "Pittsburgh on the West, Philadelphia on the East, and Alabama in-between."

The city of Pittsburgh had voted for Democrats

since the Great Depression. But, Democrat mis-management and high taxes drove Pittsburghers from the city into the boroughs of the County of Allegheny. The County slowly began to vote Republican, and that explains how Republican politicians like Bob Hill, Pat Toomey, Arlen Specter, and Richard Schweiker were elected to the U.S. Senate.

Growing up in one of America's big cities, Chris's grandfather, father and other "urban ethnics" like them, naturally voted straight Democrat. But, when they prospered and migrated to the suburbs, they increasingly voted Republican.

They were still Pittsburghers. You could tell that by their curious accent. To an outsider, it sounded as if they passed their words through their noses before expelling them from their mouths.

Chris's speech had a distinct nasal sound when he spoke that was recognizable by anyone who had spent at least a day in Pittsburgh.

And they used Pittsburgher-isms like 'Youns,' pronounced "Yinz," a pronoun used to describe others, such as in the sentence, "Yinz guys are nuts." Most non-Pittsburghers, they thought, were nuts, and Chris and his school friends shared and spoke the same sentiments in the same nasal intonations of the "Burg."

In the early 18th century, Pittsburgh was the western frontier of a growing and exuberant American nation. In the 19th and 20th centuries, it became the heart of the industrial revolution, and Chris and his fellow Pittsburghers were the benefactors of the largess of Andrew William Mellon, Henry Clay Frick, Andrew Carnegie, George Westinghouse, and H.J. Heinz.

Carnegie Library, Carnegie-Mellon University, Mellon Bank, Westinghouse Electric, the Frick Building, Frick's estate in Homestead, and later Heinz Field are vestiges of an era when there was no income tax, few federal government regulations, and no controls on the environment. When Chris' Grandfather had to attend long union organizational meetings, he took two white shirts because at midday the first one was covered with soot from the mills. That was Chris Murphy's grandfather's and his father's world.

Because Chris went to college, his world was different. Introduced to science, literature, history, art and music history, Chris devoted himself to completing his undergraduate degree. Chris gave his professors credit for knowing their academic disciplines, but he was offended by their disdain for the sports of Pittsburgh—the Pirates, Steelers, and Penguins. Some liked to hold classes on Saturday, almost daring their students to choose between "education" and Pitt Panther football games.

As a kid, Chris' Dad sold papers at the old Forbes Field across from the University of Pittsburgh's signature building, the "Cathedral of Learning." And across from the Cathedral, a multi-story warren of classrooms and offices designed as a Gothic cathedral, was the Schenley Hotel.

The Schenley Hotel, named after Mary Schenley, an heiress whose philanthropy included support of Pittsburgh charities and donations of land, among them a large tract named "Schenley Park," was built in 1898 and featured a long veranda where pedestrians could see members of visiting baseball teams sitting on rocking chairs in late afternoons before night games.

Chris Murphy's Dad would get to Forbes Field early before the beginning of night games when the teams were practicing and capture balls hit out of the park and then sell them for a dollar to parents attending that night's game. Working the park as a newspaper boy was just something that kids in Pittsburgh did back then, and if you didn't get there in time to get a clutch of papers to sell, you could buy a seat in the bleachers for a dollar.

That was an important time in America when Pittsburghers had settled-in for a life improved by the end of World War II, a growing economy, and expansion of leisure time. Ordinary working class citizens could now look forward to sending their children to college, buying a home in suburbs like Monroeville, and other ones that were developing after the war, and everyone belonged to, and regularly attended, a church or synagogue.

On his office wall, Chris had a framed photo of the Pittsburgh skyline, probably taken from what Pittsburghers called "the North Side." Eight churches are featured against a view of Downtown's commercial buildings. The photo is titled "Pittsburgh—A City of Contrasts."

One of the habits that Chris' grandfather and his father's generation of Pittsburghers shared was the custom of belonging to a church. "Where do you live?" and "What church do you belong to?" were how Pittsburghers oriented themselves to other citizens of the Burgh.

The North Side, South Side, downtown Pittsburgh and Oakland were accessible by street cars—electric trolleys—what today we call "light rail." And in those days, before beer was sold at Forbes Field, the ballpark was ringed by bars.

Pittsburgher's would arrive at Forbes Field by trolley and head for a bar. After a couple of boiler makers—a shot of whiskey and a beer—they headed to the park to celebrate their good fortune. If they didn't have tickets to the game, an Albino scalper would sell them better seats than they could have bought legally. Chris' father was fascinated by that scalper as he worked his way into Forbes Field with a clutch of papers to sell. In those days, people kept meticulous box scores and the Pittsburgh morning paper, the *Post Gazette*, sold at the game had a printed box of each inning for visitors to keep score.

Chris's Dad, despite his Irish name, was a Protestant who attended a Presbyterian church in East Liberty built by Andrew Mellon. His many Catholic friends at Pitt had attended Central Catholic High School and lived in Oakland, the North or South sides, or the Highland Park area.

Chris' favorite photo that he kept on his desk in Sen. Hill's office was a picture of his grandfather, newly returned from the War, holding his Dad in front of the monkey cage at the Highland Park Zoo.

Chris's Jewish classmates lived in Squirrel Hill and seemed more urbane, more world-wise, than his other friends. The father of one of them carried a tattoo on his left wrist, placed there when he was an infant, by guards at Auschwitz.

A sense of tragedy marked many of the families of his Dad's friends. The small community of Armenians in Pittsburgh were the offspring of survivors of a murderous rampage committed by Turks against Armenians after the collapse of the Ottoman Empire.

His Irish friends knew something about the persecution of Catholics by the British in Ireland.

Polish friends, whose parents were lucky enough to escape Poland before World War II, had encountered Polish jokes and a ghetto called Polish Hill.

The city teemed with people from countries most Americans never knew existed—Ruthenia, Croatia, Silesia—and many small towns in Germany. But each group had its church, its ethnic club, and its memories.

Chris' grandfather belonged to a German club called the "Liedertafel" that in 2014 celebrated its 130th anniversary. The Liedertafel, in Chris' grandfather's and father's day, was a private bar, much like American Legion halls, where German was spoken and the beer was brewed in the basement. The Liedertafel was a place to go after Church on Sunday.

Adjusting to an unexpected era of peace and prosperity challenged Chris in more serious ways than what his grandfather and father learned before and during World War II.

His experience as a third generation Pittsburgher led to a conflict between Chris and his professors at Pitt, and he decided that, despite his family's loyalty to the Democrats, his decision to be a Republican was the right decision.

Chris brought that inherited and learned experience to the Russell Senate Office Building on a day that radically changed his life and that of his mentor and boss, U.S. Senator Bob Hill (R-PA).

Airline pilots will tell you that an aircraft disaster isn't something that occurs just because of one event. An aircraft accident usually can be traced to a series of mistakes, of bad choices, bad training or timing, each contributing to disaster and death.

The choice of John F. Kennedy, Jr., to fly his wife in his private plane was made after only a few hours of training on instruments.

His wife's sister was late in arriving at the plane. The plane left later than Junior had planned. Nightfall disoriented him, and his reading of flight instruments failed. His uncle, Sen. Ted Kennedy, was delegated as surviving Kennedy family member to board the U.S. Grasp that was sent to pick up the pieces of the light plane and the bodies of his brother's son, wife and wife's sister.

Like John John, the lives of Sen. Bob Hill, the Senator's wife, Mary, and Chris Murphy, were about to be changed forever.

2.

U.S. Senator Bob Hill (R-PA)

Sen. Bob Hill (R-PA) came from a middle class family in Allentown in Eastern Pennsylvania, a Catholic, who had attended Harvard as an undergraduate. He attended Harvard, not St. Joseph's in Philadelphia nor Duquesne in Pittsburgh. That set him apart from other Pennsylvania Catholics.

There was also something that older folk saw in Bob Hill that they called "good instinct." He might have attended Boston College, that like St. Joe's, is a Jesuit college, but Bob had reservations about the Society of Jesus. He felt that the Jesuits were, and are today, too far to the Left of most American Catholics. Why that was the case troubled him, but he had too much to do to try and figure it out.

Chris was attracted to this politician because the Senator gave up a lucrative job as head of his family's company to run for the U.S. Senate—and he was organized. Most politicians get lucky and win election the first time they run. After that, it's all downhill. Most politicians are not interested in policy. Bob Hill was consumed by policy.

Bob Hill was also systematic in how he approached that first campaign, and Chris liked that very much. This aspiring office holder approached an election almost as if it were a new job, something with rules to obey, things to do and to master.

Sen. Hill organized his campaign more than a year before he announced his candidacy, fought a terrific campaign challenging an incumbent Republican U.S. Senator—and lost. His loss was an important lesson because none of those he had counted on to help him did.

Mainline corporations donated to the campaign of the incumbent U.S. Senator and, strapped for cash, candidate Bob Hill went down to defeat. But, it was close—47% for Bob Hill and 49% for the sitting Republican Senator.

Chris learned that "shit happens" from growing up in Pittsburgh and what, apparently, Bob Hill had also learned growing up in Allentown.

But, Bob Hill, picked himself up, and created a Tea Party organization that advocated tax relief, limited government, right to life and free enterprise. That profile was fast becoming a "fit" for Pennsylvania GOP politicians as most national Democrats moved far to the Left and, in doing so, abandoned their religious beliefs.

Unlike the citizens of Massachusetts where the Catholic church made a fateful accommodation with Kennedy Democrats, Catholics in Pennsylvania were still serious about their religious beliefs and joined millions of Protestants who also didn't like legalization of abortion. That's why they voted for Gov. Bob Casey in the face of Casey's rejection by national Democrats.

In fact, they didn't like divorce, homosexuality, marijuana, heroin, or cocaine use, though those vices had become much more common than in Chris's Dad's day.

And they really disliked taxation. Chris' generation responded to candidates for office who challenged the way that their income was diminished by taxes to support government programs initiated seventy years ago by politicians long dead.

Every time Chris looked at the withholding from his salary as a staff member of the U.S. Senate, he wondered if he was the only person of his generation who worried that Social Security, Medicare and Medicaid would severely limit his ability to prepare for retirement. Add monthly student loan payments, a home mortgage, and college for his children, and he knew something had to be done or he—and the country—would die broke. Bob Hill had come to the same conclusion and dedicated himself to tax reform and tried to figure out how to cut back on federal government entitlements without destroying his chances for election.

Many of Sen. Bob Hill's constituents were what Sen. Hill's pollster, Steve Weissman, called "urban ethnics" who later came to be known as "Reagan Democrats."

Beginning in the late 50s and early 60s, party-line Democrat voters of East and West European descent—Poles, Italians, Irish, Ukrainians—in Pittsburgh and Philadelphia moved from the inner city to the suburbs and gradually began to vote Republican.

Twenty years later, Ronald Reagan appealed to them, and thus they came to be known as "Reagan Democrats."

These "ethnic" Pole, Italian, Ukraine and Irish voters constituted a coalition consisting of business-men and Evangelical Christians who voted their pocketbooks and were fast becoming visible even to elected Republican members of what was known in

Pennsylvania as the "Stupid Party."

Republicans in Pennsylvania were not the brightest politicians in the United States. In order to win election, Bob Hill had to go beyond registered Republicans and tap into what Jerry Falwell called the "moral majority" without offending Republicans and some Democrats who liked him but not his political ideas.

Bob Hill was a quick study; in fact, he could be called an intellectual, though he knew that he shouldn't encourage that idea.

Bob Hill was a "reader." He read everything starting in the morning when he read the back of cereal boxes. He read three newspapers a day, and at night he actually read legislation on which he was expected to vote. What he read prepared him for his work as a U.S. Senator, and he enjoyed reading about the lives of generals, statesmen, and patriots who shaped the early history of the United States. He also took a shine to Bishop Fulton Sheen, whose biography he had read decades ago.

Modern intellectuals tend to be Democrats—men of the Left—who like big government and government programs, believe in total freedom of individuals to exercise their "rights," even when doing so is not right, and look down on those who are not members of the intellectual classes. They read *The New York Times*, watch MSNBC and get teary-eyed when they hear Peter, Paul, and Mary sing "Where have all the flowers gone."

So Bob Hill adopted a manner of dress and speaking that was more attuned to the majority of non-intellectual voters in his state.

He bought his suits at Sears and could be seen buying his dress shoes at discount stores or Nordstrom Rack.

Once, when he sought funds from the Defense Department to benefit some defense contractors in Pennsylvania, he prepared for his meeting with the Defense Secretary by wearing a Sears Roebuck suit, an out of style, very wide and "loud" tie, and socks of a different color.

The U.S. Secretary of Defense was a natty dresser and considered himself an "intellectual." Intentionally stumbling to make his case, Bob tricked the Secretary into figuring him for a rube so that the Secretary ended up giving him what he wanted. Bob left the Pentagon saying to himself "I suckered that bastard," and took the Metro to Union Station, walked to the Dubliner where he had a "stiff one" and then walked to his office in "Russell."

Yes, Bob Hill, along the way to election as a U.S. Senator, had developed a drinking problem, probably inherited from his Welsh forebears or that American Indian who married into his mother's family.

American Indians were not introduced to alcohol as early as Europeans, and they couldn't hold their liquor. The Welsh could, but they drank profusely. Drinking hard liquor was a cultural thing among Pennsylvania's ethnic groups and, many a night, a side table would be laden with bottles of Scotch, Bourbon, Gin, and Vodka to salute visitors to a family dinner. The fathers of Senator Bob Hill's friends were hard drinkers. They passed that on to their sons.

There's a tale to be told about what Bob learned, related to what you do when living with an alcoholic. Bob's Dad drank heavily and had been changed, his mother said, by World War II. When he was sober, family life was peaceful. And when he drank, he was an angry and loud drunk. Bob learned not to cross his Dad and to avoid him when he was drinking. At an early age, Bob avoided confrontation by playing baseball or tag football with friends, or reading a book that he picked up at the local library. And he had a terrific gift for telling jokes—all these—baseball, reading, and jokes were learned ways of avoiding confrontation.

Despite the hurt they hid, Bob came to understand that his story and joke-telling was a great benefit to an aspiring politician.

His reading was eclectic, and by picking up books here and there he learned a lot about the history of the American Navy and the career of John Paul Jones, about the sweep of Western civilization from Hendrick van Loon. He was also attracted to poetry, especially the poetry of Robert Frost and T.S. Eliot. That reading unleashed his love for words and affected his ability to think, to size up a situation quickly and avoid confrontation. All were to become assets in his political career.

Senator Bob Hill noticed that most of his colleagues in the U.S. Senate had some of the same gifts. They could size up anyone they met in a split-second. It was a gift that helped them to survive national politics.

Senator Hill could be "earthy," and regularly used profanity in private.

His father's mother died when he was three, and his father sent him to live with his brother's family in Philadelphia until he, Bob's father, could put his life back together. He became street smart, a tough little kid who knew how to fight and curse. When he returned home after his father married again, his brother refused to walk home from school with him because every other word he spoke was a profanity. "Fuck," "shit," "mother fucker" were interspersed with keen obser- vations about his surroundings—at age ten!

In private, every other word Senator Hill spoke would have offended a longshoreman. But in public, Sen. Bob Hill was known for not giving offense. He avoided confrontation, and he made himself likeable— to voters, his Congressional colleagues and members of the Republican National Committee (RNC)—to whom Senator Bob Hill was considered "loyal."

His likeability had limits, however. When there was no other way of dealing with a situation, he dug in and fought to win.

"Senator," Chris Murphy said, "Here's the text of your speech to the…"

"Chris, I don't need any God damn speech for these bastards."

"Yes, Senator, but your wife will be with you, and you know she's your biggest critic."

"Chris, I still don't need that damn speech, but I could use a drink."

U.S. Senators today, and some Cabinet Secretaries in the old days, kept private bars in their offices and used liquor as a way to mend fences, get along with people they despised, or just relax after a long day of hearings or meetings with constituents.

Senator Bob Hill preferred constituents over lobbyists and actually liked going to events organized by his fellow Pennsylvanians, but he didn't mind taking a trip or two that lobbyists organized, especially at Augusta or to attend the World Series where these "trips" were spiced with pitches for legislation and served with drinks.

Bob Hill had started with beer in college. After college he switched to bourbon, and when he was in his thirties he switched to Scotch.

By the time he ran for office in his forties, he was drinking Gin. But Gin smelled and created the wrong impression, so he switched to Vodka. He knew that was a dangerous change in habit, but he loved the feeling that a Vodka martini gave him.

This particular day was cold in Washington, DC, and that night it could have snowed, so Senator Bob Hill prepared for his upcoming event by walking to his liquor cabinet, pouring a shot of vodka, and taking some ice from a mini-freezer when he was interrupted by Chris Murphy.

"If you're going to make that speech, you'll have to leave now, Senator." Sen. Hill took a sip of his drink and carefully placed it in the mini-freezer. He'd need it after the speech.

"Senator, I'll have the car outside in ten minutes. A speech, if you choose to use one, is in the inside pocket of your jacket."

"I know you'll be too busy to read this in advance, but there's a section in the speech that's critical of the Patriot Act and calls for not sending ground troops into Syria. Your constituents haven't been prepared for this, so this speech launches your attempt to distance yourself from Senator Walker and the Neoconservatives.

Bob Hill was itching to do that. Senator Walker was a big government Republican. And when the Senator began to win votes by calling for intervention in other countries where foreign governments abused their people, Sen. Hill wondered where the national interest could be found by running off to make other people safe for democracy.

3.

Mary Hill, Senate Wife

Mary Hill was known by her friends as "one tough lady." Consequently, she didn't much like being categorized as a "Senate Wife" but, that's how wives of Senators are categorized.

Raised near Pittsburgh in the Monongahela Valley, she came from a family of coal miners. When she was born, her family lived in a shack that had dirt floors, water from a pump, and an outhouse.

The "Mon" valley was a tough place to grow up, but there were public schools and football teams that graduated the likes of Mike Ditka who went to Pitt and played for the Steelers and Joe Montana who went to Notre Dame and won a national championship and played for the San Francisco '49rs and Joe Namath who played for Alabama and the New York Jets.

Religion, specifically the Catholic Church, was very important to Mrs. Hill, or she would have divorced Sen.

Hill years ago.

She loved him, but she couldn't stand his reliance on alcohol to get him through each session of Congress.

Mary Hill prayed for her husband by saying the Rosary as many as fifty times a day and looked forward to returning "home" whenever she could. Though saying the Rosary was in response to her life with the Senator, even if she hadn't married Bob Hill, the Rosary would still have been something she did, just because that was her nature.

The popular description of people like Mary Hill is that they are "sensitive souls." The clinical way to describe her—if clinics today were open to religion—was to say that she had frequent mystic experiences.

William James wrote about that in *Varieties of Religious Experience*, and much that he wrote explained Mary Hill's nature. Mary was simply open to God's talking to her. It began when she was about ten and prayed to Jesus asking if she might see his face. She was shocked to hear him say, "What have you done to earn that?" But, she was not shocked to hear his voice.

She reacted to this experience by resolving to earn Jesus' love and developed a number of methods beginning with the Rosary. Sometimes, she reflected on the words, and other times she repeated the words by rote.

She began to pray to Saints and even prayed to some recently deceased relatives who were believers and lived lives worthy of the name "Catholic."

One Saint in particular occupied her prayer life: Saint Patrick, the Saint of second chances. There was something that attracted her to him especially as the chaos of her husband's political career gave her an understanding that in life there are no straight lines.

Ruby, her black classmate at Ringgold Middle School in Monongahela, Pennsylvania, would say to her that "all things occur for a reason," and Mary somehow knew that she would need spiritual resources to endure the bad things that would certainly come.

Prayer was her way of preparing.

All this is explained by contemporary psychology as typical attitudes of lower class men and women. If you show them a picture of someone with his hands on his face, a lower class person will say, "he's crying." A middle class person will say, "he's keeping the sun out of his eyes." Mary Hill knew better. Jesus' rebuke was a challenge for her to earn the right to see him face-to-face.

Mary's father worked at U.S. Steel's Blast Furnace plant in Duquesne and moved his family to Swissvale, Pennsylvania. In 1996, at the age of 17, she was able to earn her high school diploma from Swissvale High School, and though her family couldn't afford to send her to college, she qualified for scholarships and Pell grants and was admitted to the University of Pittsburgh.

Twenty-five years ago, Pitt wasn't building its future by servicing "locals" or their religious, political or economic interests, so Mary had to be exceptionally talented even to be admitted.

As a "townie," Mary was able to return home to her family each night and share some of her experiences with her classmates and professors. More important, she would attend Mass in her home parish every Sunday or at St. Paul's Cathedral in Oakland, near Pitt's Cathedral of Learning.

St. Paul's Cathedral was "home" to Pittsburgh's Catholics. Built in 1906 by Chicago architects James Egan and Charles Prindeville, St. Paul's is rivaled by the East Liberty Presbyterian Church completed in 1935 by architect Ralph Adams Cram.

Cram specialized in Protestant church architecture and Egan in Catholic. St. Paul's had the advantage of location in the heart of Oakland, Pittsburgh's cultural center across from the University of Pittsburgh. East Liberty Presbyterian was, unfortunately, located in East Liberty. Though at the time the Cathedral was constructed, East Liberty was a thriving community bordered by the communities of Highland Park and Shadyside. East Liberty had shops, including a cafeteria and a Greek candy store. It also featured a high rise building with an arcade, and the Enright theater named after the first Pittsburgher killed in World War I.

The many wars of the 20th century shaped Pittsburgh, and so many streets were named after battles that one wag asked if World War II was fought in Pittsburgh. Life in the Burg was good for a very long time, but the steel industry that fueled Pittsburgh rapidly declined, and East Liberty fell into decay. The parish community that supported the Presbyterian Cathedral no longer exists.

Though Mary was proud of being a student at Pitt, she was troubled, as was her husband, by the political views of her professors and their disdain for the religious heritage of the communities that surrounded it. The University "milked" local ethnic groups for the financing to fund "nationality" rooms, but did nothing to assure that their history or religions were honored in the university's academic departments. A subsidiary benefit of this bias was to confirm Mary in her Catholic faith, and she increased the frequency of praying the Rosary each day.

There was something about the Virgin Mary that resonated with Mary, and she came to appreciate that her parents gave her the same name. Protestants pray to Jesus, and Jewish believers to the God of Israel, but Catholics are attracted to the mother of Jesus.

What Mary found was that Mary's Intercessions led to answers of her prayers.

Her mother was suddenly stricken by a stroke and Mary begged the Virgin Mary to intercede so that God would spare her mother. On another occasion, Mary was not able to pay her tuition. She prayed for help from the Virgin Mary, and somehow Pitt found a scholarship to cover tuition cost for her last year of studies. The relationship with the Virgin Mary was sealed by those events, and Mary came to enjoy repeating the Rosary as many times a day as she had time.

At Pitt, Mary Hill, worked part time as a secretary for the Physical Education Department and commuted to school, first by bus and later by driving a 1954 Chevy that a neighbor gave her. The Department let her park at Pitt Stadium, so she spent lots of energy walking up what people from the Plains States would call a mountain. That car used more oil than gas, but it gave her the freedom of driving to school as opposed to taking a bus.

Pittsburgh continues to have good public transportation developed in days before families had cars. And after considering the cost of parking downtown, many professionals still use the bus. Mary preferred to drive, and that was the other aspect of Mary's personality that her friends noticed.

Mary Hill loved freedom and hated dependency, Freedom of movement, of thought, of religion, and freedom to choose what she wanted to study meant everything to Mary. But how should she use that freedom at Pitt? That concerned her when, after choosing to become a Philosophy major, she found that the Philosophy Department was as modern and secular as any in higher education.

The History Department was dramatically Left-wing and was said to have harbored a Communist Party cell. The Department of Economics was dedicated to defending the New Deal and Keynesian to the core. She might have chosen Classics, but that beleaguered Department was small, and there were no career paths that Mary could see by keeping up her Latin or learning classical Greek.

She had little interest in Biology or Chemistry and

loved the law, so Mary chose the Political Science Department hoping that would lead to admission to law school and a career as an attorney.

Much to her dismay, the Political Science Department was deeply committed to "value free" social science that studied human "behavior" and ignored the moral dimension of human action. Mary ridiculed this approach as "comparative rectangles." So Mary found solace by taking as many courses in the English Department as she could work into her degree program. As a result, she developed an attractive prose style and came to love the poetry of T. S. Eliot and Robert Frost, and she was intrigued also by the poems of Rainer Maria Rilke. That, in a funny way, was what attracted Mary to Bob Hill.

One poem that they both liked was titled "Birches." "Still without shadow, shot through with light, like a stand of birches in early April..." and she was delighted that, on a fact-finding trip to Germany with her husband, she experienced a forest of ashen white birch trees.

It was quite uncommon for a young woman from Swissvale to enjoy poetry and English literature, but the Pitt English Department hosted two very distinguished professors of English.

In Mary's first year at Pitt, she took a course from Shakespearian scholar, Charles Crow, and yet another in Poetry. Crow was esteemed by his colleagues, but his students especially enjoyed his meticulous reading of their papers, each folded horizontally with the student's name and title of his or her paper at the right top of the first page. Mary was fortunate because after she took his courses, Charles Crow retired.

The other influence on her appreciation of literature was Richard Tobias. Tobias had been teaching at Pitt for fifteen years when Mary enrolled, and she enjoyed taking several of his classes. One in particular stoked her love of poetry. 'Tudor Prose and Poetry' was an undergraduate course that offered an opportunity to study Renaissance literature without the skepticism that seeped into those studies in the Philosophy and History Departments. Edmund Spenser's "Fairie Queen" enchanted her and led her to read Richard Hooker's Ecclesiastical Polity.

She found the introduction to that tome relevant to late 20th century America as it rapidly was transformed from a republic into a nation-state. Richard Hooker's admonition that we must not forget "as through a glass darkly" the history of the times about which he wrote inspired her to read widely in English and American history.

Pittsburgh in 1996, like the United States, was undergoing a transition. The "Burg" had lost much of its population to the suburbs. With close to 600,000 residents in 1960, by the 1990s the city of Pittsburgh had declined to fewer than 300,000. Much was made of a renewal by business leaders in the late 1950s, but like most urban renewals, the Pittsburgh "Renaissance" disrupted large areas where people had lived, particularly those who lived in the "Hill District."

Mary's father would tell her about the wonderful Syrian bread that was baked daily at a bakery near where the Civic Center was built, and he would tell her about ice skating at the Duquesne Gardens in Oakland where the Pittsburgh Hornets, predecessor to the Penguins, played. And Forbes Field was mentioned whenever he took time to reflect on the Pittsburgh of the "old days."

Mary's memories of Pittsburgh were on a continuum of memories shared by her parents. In many ways, Mary lived in the past and enjoyed life lived today from the perspective of how it once was as told to her by her parents.

4.

A Doubling of Grace

Apollonia is a feminine name derived from the Greek "Apollonius" and Apollo the god of sunlight, son of Zeus and Leto. In Catholic church history, Saint Apollonia was a Christian martyred in third century AD when she did not renounce her faith.

Apollonia McCarthy was of Greek/Irish descent and named Apollonia because her mother's family came from the Greek island of Kos located off the Anatolian coast of Turkey. The village of Kardamena on Kos is popular with young people from the UK and Scandinavia. Apollonia and Mary Hill grew up together in Western Pennsylvania in different suburbs of Pittsburgh.

Mary grew up in the suburb of Swissvale and Apollonia in Braddock. Her father, like Mary's, worked in the mills. That she was of Greek and Irish descent was unusual, if only because the number of Pitts-

41

burghers of Greek descent was small. Resistance to intermarriage between Irish and Italian Catholics had been overcome by late-20th century, and resistance to marrying a non-Greek soon followed. There were two Roman Catholic churches for Irish-Americans in Braddock, St. William and St. Brendan.

But when Apollonia began to attend Pitt, she chose to attend St. Nikolas Greek Orthodox Cathedral, near the campus in Oakland. She couldn't explain why, but there was something drawing her to a ritual that celebrated the God who was everywhere present.

By the time Mary Hill was admitted to the University of Pittsburgh, she preferred to attend St. Paul's Cathedral a block from Pitt's Cathedral of Learning. Before Vatican II, Catholics riding to work on Pittsburgh's street cars would make the sign of the cross as they passed St. Paul's open doors.

The University of Pittsburgh, more than the public schools in Swissvale and Braddock, shaped Mary's and Apollonia's future lives. Swissvale public schools were terrible, as were those in Braddock. These boroughs served working class families and few knew anything about their children's teachers whose principal job was to warehouse them until they could legally leave school and find work in the mills. That motivated both girls to excel in school in order to escape. Apollonia loved Mathematics, Chemistry, and Biology and knew that she wanted to be a physician.

Both Mary and Apollonia spent their time at Pitt in classes, studying and commuting home from university. They did that for four years when Apollonia was admitted to Pitt's medical school and Mary found the love of her life, an aspiring young and politically ambitious, Bob Hill.

Apollonia's career dictated her life and she never married. Though their lives and careers went in different directions, they spoke to one another at least once a year and quickly learned to text when that technology was introduced. Apollonia last texted her the day before Mary Hill was killed.

5.

Road to the White House

Ohio and Pennsylvania are key states in Presidential elections. George H. W. Bush and Donald Trump were the only Republicans to win both Ohio and Pennsylvania, Bush in 1988 and Trump in 2016. George W. Bush won Ohio in 2000 but lost to Al Gore in Pennsylvania. So there had been a long drought during which Republicans lost Presidential elections largely because of poor showings in Ohio and Pennsylvania.

Bob Hill and George Walker knew that their states were critical to election of Presidents. Both were ambitious politicians who didn't think that the duties of President of the United States were beyond their ability. It was inevitable that their ambitions would clash and the Presidential election of 2024 was the event that would challenge them both.

The Republican Presidential nomination would be won by the candidate who promised to unify the Republican Party after the Party had broken down into factions in 2016 and 2020. The election of 2016 saw an outsider win the GOP nomination by defeating a formidable cast of Republican politicians and also revealed that the American two-party system was about to fragment.

The last realignment of major political parties in the United States occurred after the Kansas-Nebraska Act of 1854 forced the issue of slavery to the forefront of American politics. The Whig Party led by Henry Clay and John Tyler was split, and an anti-slavery faction was formed that nominated Abraham Lincoln for President. From the time of Lincoln's presidency, American politics was dominated by Republicans and Democrats, but in 2016 the Republican Party was in such disrepair that it elected a person largely chosen because he was a marketing genius. His lack of know-ledge of government exacerbated by dyslexia brought the GOP to near extinction. By the time Bob Hill and Charles Walker sought the Presidency, what was left of the Republican Party was energized by the two can-didates' hatred of one another.

After the defeat of John McCain (R-AZ) to Barack Obama (R-IL) in 2008, though 146 million Americans lived in all-GOP states compared to 49 million in all-Democratic states, Republicans lost the Presidential elections of 2008 and 2012.

In 2010, the GOP quickly regained control of the U.S. House of Representatives, but the damage done by the 110th Congress controlled by Democrats was complete. President Obama managed to introduce and pass the Affordable Care Act that affirmed universal healthcare as a right, rather than a personal responsibility, and the 110th Congress went on a spending binge "investing" in "shovel ready" programs that did little to recover from the economic recession caused by the banking crisis of 2008.

The effects of the Banking crisis of 2008 lingered well into President Obama's second term and real economic growth in GDP of 2.38% was the slowest recovery since 1930-1933.

In the election of 2010, the GOP regained control of the U.S. House of Representatives largely from a revolt by new entrants into elective politics called the "Tea Party." Their revolt continued, and in 2015 the GOP captured control of the U.S. Senate, but the GOP controlled Congress did nothing. Cong. John Boehner

(R-OH) who secured the House Speakership with Tea Party support in 2010 became a casualty in 2015 when it became apparent that Boehner was incapable of leading an aggressive attack on President Obama and his Congressional Democrats.

Ohio politicians like John Boehner revealed how deep were Ohio's roots in the mindset of the "moderate" Liberal wing of the GOP.

Boehner believed that his responsibility was to assure that the legislative process was stable, not to lead a counter-revolution. Sen. Rob Portman (R-OH) was firmly committed to doing nothing as well, and Gov. John Kasich never saw a government program he didn't like nor one that he felt he could improve by making it his own.

On the Senate-side of the Republican Congressional majority, the Senate Majority Leader, Mitch McConnell, talked a good game but never acted in a consistent way to reverse growth of government programs and expansion of Executive powers. Sen. Rand Paul successfully challenged the McConnell machine in Kentucky, was elected to the U.S. Senate in 2011, but couldn't raise sufficient interest in his candidacy for President.

The time was ripe for change, yet Republican Speaker of the House John Boehner (R-OH) and Republican Senate Majority leader Mitch McConnell (R-KY) failed to respond aggressively to a host of important issues that defined the differences between the Republicans and Democrats.

The Grand Old Party was simply too old, and no new leaders revived its prospects.

President Obama's National Security policy was badly managed and ineffective in addressing the threat of Islamic terrorism. A treaty with Iran, arguably the worst treaty with any foreign government in American history, assigned hegemony in the Arab states, India, and Pakistan to the Islamic regime in Iran and halted Iran's nuclear weapons program only on paper.

Though the federal deficit was reduced by means of "sequestration" authorized in the Budget Control Act of 2011, without budget reforms affecting Entitlements the national debt would soon exceed 100% of GDP.

The American economy was still in recession, yet President Obama's aversion to working with Congress led him to govern through executive orders and some-thing called "negotiated rulemaking."

According to George Washington University's regulatory studies center, the Obama administration in its first seven years finalized 560 major regulations, nearly 50 percent more than the George W. Bush administration during the comparable period. The Obama Administration also used a little known power of "negotiated rule-making" to create federal regulations without seeking Congressional approval.

This "Executive overreach" justified instituting a resolution for Impeachment, but even that was beyond the capacity of Congressional Republicans who exhibited overwhelming "white guilt" that deterred them from forcefully challenging an African American President.

None of the professional politicians who campaigned for the GOP nomination in 2016 could overcome the public's decision to choose an outsider. A celebrity businessman won the nomination, and even though he did not wage a professionally managed campaign for President, he defeated his Democrat opponent.

Both Bob Hill and George Walker saw opportunity in the GOP's defeat in the 2018 and 2020 Congressional elections and felt that they could turn defeat into victory. The election of 2024 was their opportunity to succeed a two-term President. Both began to prepare for a run for the White House.

After his career was salvaged by reelection to the United States Senate in 2020, Bob Hill began to plan his first run for President and approached that task in characteristic organized fashion. He carefully developed ties to conservative policy advocates in national security, tax, and regulatory policy and entitlement reform.

Bob Hill had decided that we either did something about entitlements or the entire economy would collapse. He decided to touch the electric "Third Rail" and planned to run on a platform of Entitlement reform. Bob could be seen visiting the headquarters of the Heritage Foundation and Cato Institute where he met with experts in economics, and he huddled with Art Laffer, Richard Rahn, and other advocates of supply-side Economics.

Bob Hill's affection for the legacy of Ronald Reagan led him to get to know Richard Allen, then age 85, Reagan's first National Security Advisor, Dr. John Lehman, age 74, former Secretary of the Navy in the Reagan Administration and Dr. William Schneider, age 75, former Undersecretary of State for Security Policy.

Bob Hill was now 45, having entered first grade when Reagan made his third run for the GOP nomination in 1980, but he remembered his Dad telling him about how the Reagan Administration was split between conservative "hard liners" and "pragmatists" who wanted nothing to do with many of the policies that Ronald Reagan championed during the three times he ran for President.

All three, Allen, Lehman, and Schneider were hard line "cold warriors" who opposed granting concessions to the Soviet Union, and that all were Catholics was important for a Senator from Pennsylvania desiring to become President.

Dick Allen was a graduate of Notre Dame, John Lehman graduated from St. Joseph's College in Philadelphia, and Bill Schneider went to New York University.

They knew one another from the Goldwater campaign in 1964 and had experienced the bitter taste of defeat. Bob Hill, they believed, had a shot at becoming President. But, it was more important to them that he was committed to limited government than to party unity. After the 2020 Presidential election, there was a realignment of factions within the GOP and in the electorate, and Bob Hill, they felt, could play a significant role rallying traditional conservatives and Steve

Weisman's "urban ethnics" into becoming a force once again within the GOP.

All three, Allen, Lehman and Schneider were also opposed to moderate politicians who, throughout their careers, softened the foreign and national security policy positions of Richard Nixon, Gerald Ford, and later, the Gipper. They were especially frustrated by George W. Bush's "shoot first and aim later" approach that involved the United States in a disastrous war in Iraq.

Bob Hill assembled these old men in his Russell Senate Office building quarters in 2019 because he wanted to tap their experience and knowledge. Bob Hill couldn't personally acquire their experience, but he wanted the knowledge that experience had taught them.

"Can I offer you a drink?" Senator Hill asked.

Dick Allen used to enjoy drinks with Secretary of Defense Melvin Laird (R-WI) during Nixon's first term. A former eight-term Congressman, Laird served in the House when relations between members were not drowned by political correctness. Most politicians fifty, or even forty, years ago were "interest oriented" and could be moved to support an opponent's legislation if it didn't conflict with their own interests.

Having a drink in a well-equipped office was one of the ways that Laird exerted leadership in the House even though his Party was in the minority.

Allen, Lehman, and Schneider accepted the invitation for a drink. Lehman eyed a bottle of Jack Daniels in the first row of lubricants in Hill's well-stocked bar, and Allen and Schneider chose Scotch. All were old enough to go through the progression from beer to bourbon to scotch, gin, and then vodka, but that afternoon Bob chose to drink Jack Daniels with Lehman.

Lehman sipped the sour mash whiskey, remembering days when he was young and the future of America and the GOP looked so appealing. He preferred lighter stuff, but disdained white wine as a drink for Liberals. If he was going to advise a Presidential aspirant, he may as well drink what he drinks.

"Here are the four issues that are on my mind and I hope you can get me oriented to do what's in the national interest," said Bob Hill.

"Number One," Bob Hill began. He liked to lay things out by numbering them, because it sounded as if he had thought things out. Often, however, he was speaking off the top of his head and covered his extemporaneity by counting.

"The international wing of the GOP killed the Republican brand—and a lot of good soldiers—with a reckless pursuit of democracy in foreign lands. These guys hate 'dictators' and want us to intervene in every tragic situation in the world. Bosnia, Iraq, Libya were places where we didn't need to intervene but we did. Somehow, we need to build arguments for staying home without sounding like isolationists."

"Number two, what are our real military needs, and is there any way to control the military services from empire building? I don't believe we need more aircraft carriers, but I worry that—in the absence of space-based defenses—our submarine force is not an adequate deterrent."

"Number three, what specifically is missing in our defenses? What defenses should we prepare now to meet threats from the PRC, Iran, and Russia?"

"And, number four, how can we get away from this fucking feminization thing?" Bob intentionally added the profanity for effect.

"Placing women in combat positions is dangerous and places our fighting men at risk."

As Bob Hill spoke, his guests looked at one another. They couldn't believe what they were hearing.

Finally, here was a politician who saw national security in realistic terms and without the ideological baggage of Liberal Republicans and the Leftist ideology of Democrats that clouded their thinking about national security.

The Presidential election campaign in 2024 was shaping to be a fight between Sen. Hill and Sen. Walker. Bob Hill looked at it as a fight for the soul of the Republican Party.

Both knew that the President, going on 81, was weakened by age and a weak economy. After another Banking crisis, a Covid-19 pandemic, collapse of the Stock Market, difficult supplies of parts originally sourced from the PRC, the American economy was facing economic "stagnation."

Bob Hill was younger than the incumbent by over thirty years. The only wild card in his speculation was the status of the economy over national security. Economic issues were uppermost, not the military issues that concerned Bob Hill. Yet, Bob Hill was convinced that the next President would be challenged by enemies much like John F. Kennedy was challenged by the Soviet Union's Nikita Khrushchev. His plan was to get elected with a plan prepared to deal with what was coming in terms of national defense.

Sen. George Walker approached this election in terms of more immediate concerns. His pollster, George Eisen, had conducted surveys that indicated what problems Republican primary voters were concerned about and there were three—the same concerns that propelled his candidate into the U.S. Senate in 2016: open borders, slow economic growth, foreign trade.

"The Wall" promised by the President had not been built, and lack of enforcement of immigration laws allowed even more illegals to enter the United States. The only thing that stopped the flow was improvement in the Mexican economy, largely the result of investments in manufacturing by American companies fleeing American taxes that the President couldn't lower due to Congressional Democrats.

Having promised more spending on old and new programs, little had been done since the President's tax reforms of 2018 to foster economic growth by lowering taxes. Tax cuts were granted to persons with annual incomes of between $50,000 and $80,000, but raising taxes of the wealthy to 70% didn't spur investment in new enterprises. Americans felt that they were getting poorer and wanted to see an economy that grew GDP by 3% a year, not the 1.5% growth in recent years.

And though Americans enjoyed their low-priced televisions and other gadgets, they also wanted to see manufacturing return to places like Dayton, Pittsburgh, Ft. Wayne, Flint, and other former centers of manufacturing. George Walker had plans to grow manufacturing in his home town of Dayton and made those plans central to his election campaign.

Bob Hill was popular in Pittsburgh where new industries that were developing in the Burgh were intellectual and "sweat-equity" based.

Google was transforming whole areas that once devastated the inner city, and Uber had introduced "self-driving" vehicles in Pittsburgh—the first in the nation.

Carnegie Mellon University attracted the brightest technically-gifted students from around the world, and many stayed after graduation and started businesses that their families financed.

They were from places like India, Taiwan and the People's Republic of China, and they wanted to stay in the United States. George Walker introduced legislation that allowed them to stay.

With George Eisen's advice, Walker threw into this policy mix some red meat for Americans who felt threatened by immigrants.

He called for reductions in the immigration of Muslims and a tax on foreign financed startups. If foreign financing of new enterprises exceeded 51%, Walker called for a 5% levy on income generated by the new companies. He also called for a 30% tariff on goods entering the United States manufactured by American companies.

A Buick engine manufactured in the People's Republic of China was made the object of this new legislation.

"Why," Walker asked, "should GM manufacture engines for Buicks in some other country. Aren't our workers good enough?"

6.

The End of the Beginning

Early that December morning, Chris Murphy arrived at the office of Sen. Hill in the Russell Senate Office Building, made some final edits to his Senator's speech, and placed a copy in the Senator's suit jacket.

George O Walker was a bully, which was another reason Bob Hill wanted to defeat Walker's plans for a run for the GOP nomination for President of the United States.

He turned to his chief of staff and said, "Chris, I'm going to knock the shit out of Walker's fucking foreign policy."

Bob Hill put on his suit jacket, felt the pages of the speech that Chris Murphy insisted he use, left his office and headed to the elevator reserved for Senators about five paces away. This was an important meeting for Senator Hill because he wanted to prepare his consti-tuents and the Washington political classes for a very "un" Republican attitude toward war.

America's role in the world, he believed, and the purposes of military force was not to make the world democratic, nor to redress the many wrongs inflicted on citizens by foreign rulers. The role of the United States in world politics was to assure that the United States remained independent and that no one country dominated all other countries in a region. Iran, China and Russia, from that perspective, had to be watched very carefully and American interests—and those of our allies in the Middle East, Asia and Europe—defended.

That meant sustaining a military position in Asia and Western Europe that America had inherited from World War II, but mindful that the national interest of the United States was to achieve a balance of power and resist domination of our allies. South Korea, the Republic of China, and Japan were threatened by the PRC, the Baltic states and Poland by Russia, and south Asia by Iran.

That clarified for Senator Hill the limits of U.S. power and made him skeptical of foreign policies that used America's power to achieve goals not central to our national interest. While these nations in south Asia sorted out the disruption of the balance of power in the

Middle East that was the result of American destruction of the regime of Saddam Hussein in Iraq, Senator Hill thought it best to keep the U.S. out of that conflict.

"Leave the fucking wogs alone to fight among themselves," he said.

Republicans love the U.S. Military.

Senator Hill liked them, too, which is why he was going to take a position at this next speaking event against using American armed forces for non-strategic purposes.

Somewhere along the way, probably in reading about American history, Senator Bob Hill developed an understanding of balance of power and saw the world in terms of "Internationalists," what he called "fucking do-gooders" and "nationalists."

Arriving at the Senate garage from the elevator, Sen. Hill spotted his car, driven by Chris Murphy, and Mary Hill sitting in the front seat of the car. Mary Hill, Sen. Bob Hill's wife, was a front seat driver extraordinaire.

Once, Sen. Hill had to stop driving and invite his wife to leave the car. She never did, nor on this important day did she give up her front seat.

"There you are!" she said. "I got here a full fifteen

minutes ago, and you were to start speaking in ten minutes. Get your ass moving."

The drive from Russell to the Mayflower Hotel took no more than fifteen minutes, but Bob Hill used those minutes to shape what he was going to say at the event organized by the American Enterprise Institute. He didn't need Chris' "damn speech" to say what was on his mind.

The American Enterprise Institute, what everyone called "AEI," was founded in the 1940s by a Lebanese American, Bill Baroody, Sr. It quickly became a vehicle for corporations to exercise soft influence in Washington by sponsoring policy studies, so AEI fast developed into what came to be known as the first free enterprise "Think Tank." Baroody developed close ties to the Eisenhower Administration, and AEI became a kind of government in exile for former Nixon Administration appointees during the Kennedy and Johnson Administrations.

AEI in those days was a bastion of Republican orthodoxy until Bill Sr. died and Irving Kristol pushed Bill Baroody, Jr., out. Under the influence of Irving Kristol, AEI took a Neoconservative tack.

Baroody had mistakenly thought he could work with the Neocons in Washington, milk their influence, and keep control of AEI. But, "Senior" found that when the issue of succession arose, the Neocons were not inclined to accept Senior's choice of his son, Bill, Jr. Junior was ousted and thus began development of a bastion of Neoconservative influence that came to dominate the second term of Ronald Reagan and reached critical mass during the administration of George W. Bush.

As Sen. Hill and his wife entered the lobby of the Mayflower Hotel, they encountered a flurry of activity as his host's intern escorted him into the ballroom where he would speak.

A majestic old hotel centrally located in downtown DC on Connecticut Avenue, the Mayflower was built in 1925 when many guests travelled with servants. Today, the cheaper rooms are actually the small quarters where in the old days "the help" slept.

Calvin Coolidge's Inaugural Ball was held at the Mayflower, and in the 1960s, the editors of Human Events held the first "Conservative Political Action Conferences" at the Mayflower. That became "CPAC" thirty years later. J. Edgar Hoover and Clyde Tolson ate dinner every night at Harveys, located next to the Mayflower, except Wednesday when they ate at Blackies. The power lunch was born at Harveys and

Blackies and was surpassed only by Duke Zeibert's and later Mel Krupin's restaurant down the street at Connecticut and L NW.

As Senator Hill entered the Mayflower ballroom, he spotted familiar faces and began shaking hands. He would have reached out to others, but the band struck a march, the attendees stood up, and Sen. Hill headed to the dais.

The Master of Ceremonies of this AEI event was a younger staff person, Stony Brooks, largely unknown to most of the attendees at this event and chosen in order not to suggest endorsement of the non Neo-conservative views of Sen. Hill.

"I'm pleased," said Stony, "to introduce the guiding light of traditional conservative forces in the United States Senate, Senator Robert Hill of Pennsylvania and his wife, Mary."

Sen. Hill rose from his chair, walked to the dais, gulped a glass of water and said, "Thank you very much Stony. I'm pleased to bring the light of traditional limited government to the darkness of AEI."

From the audience, Sen. Hill could hear murmurs, and that spurred him to begin with criticism of AEI. He began his speech as the leaders of the war faction within the GOP listened quietly.

"Let me speak from the heart. At critical times in our country's history, the American people elected Senators and Presidents who addressed the reality of this nation's spirit. I believe that since the end of the New Deal and beginning in the Administration of President Harry Truman the American people have been seeking to walk away from a government that taxed them to death, sent their children to die in foreign wars to create a New World Order, used the powers of the state to spy on American citizens, and made Americans feel bad because they were happy, making a decent living, and prayed to God.

"Many of those great men were less than perfect. So whenever someone extols my virtues, I try to remember that I'm just as outraged as everyone else—no more, no less. [Laughter]

"The leadership that America needs today is much greater than when the founder of my Party, Abraham Lincoln, brought his leadership to our country to counter the evils of Civil War that were at hand.

"How many years ago was that? Close to one hundred and sixty years? And today we are more divided as a people—and a Party—than we were then. The nation is on a trajectory leading toward bankruptcy from over-spending. The nation is divided by foreign wars pursued for the wrong reasons, and most reasonable Americans understand that we are facing a cultural crackup.

"You and I agree only that we are facing a cultural crackup. We do not agree on the use of military power to make other countries democratic. And we do not agree that Americans love government, nor do we agree that we should expand government every time we achieve power.

"I ask each and every one of you to think about that, and ask yourself what are the solutions this country needs and on which can we agree?

"I know, this is the last year in the President's first term, but we've got to begin now to ask whether we want more of the same, or whether we can do better.

"Thank you and remember that we all have to work together or those Liberal bastards will win."

That last bit of salty language generated laughter and modest applause as the Senator left the dais, met his wife and walked through the throng toward their car. Chris Murphy's cell phone rang and the young driver answered. "Hello, sure honey what's up?" "You what?" "Now?" "I'm on my way, give me fifteen minutes to get there."

As he shut his cell phone, Chris spied Mary Hill and

explained that he can't drive the Senator and wife, but has to get his wife to the delivery room at George Washington Hospital.

"I understand," Chris, "take care of your wife, but give me the keys to the car, and I'll handle the Senator."

Sen. Hill's exit from the Mayflower slowed as he reached for a drink from a passing waiter. His wife, angered by the delay, said "Come on, Senator, these people need to eat their dinner, and we have to meet the Hansens at the Palm."

"Okay, honey. One quick tour of the room as we head out the door, okay?"

"Alright, I'll be downstairs. Chris had to take his wife to GW Hospital, but the car is waiting downstairs."

There was a flurry of activity of guests greeting the Senator as he made his way to the ballroom exit, walked toward an escalator, and arrived at the exit where Mary Hill was impatiently waiting.

"Give me the keys, " he said. "Are you sure?" she asked.

"Never better. Besides I know how to get there fast."

Sen. Hill took the keys, opened the door for his wife, and took the wheel of the car and drove up Connecticut Avenue when he made the first left turn. Just as he turned, a car driving down Connecticut

Avenue slammed into the passenger side of the car, throwing Mrs. Hill through the windshield.

Senator Hill awakened in the Emergency Room of George Washington University Hospital, groggy and bleeding from a broken nose.

"Mary! Where's Mary?"

7.

A Day in Court

Defendants in the District of Columbia's Courts will find they are not alone, and on this day Sen. Bob Hill, three attorneys, and six members of his Senate staff awaited sentencing with an audience of some 100 defendants and several hundred observers.

Courtroom 115 in the DC/Traffic Community Court in the Moultrie Courthouse can handle at least 100 defendants who collectively plead guilty. Located in the Judiciary Square area of downtown Washington, DC, however, the area is notable for a lack of public parking. Most defendants lost their license to drive, so parking is not a concern.

On this day, Sen. Bob Hill was sentenced on three counts: DUI, vehicular homicide, and driving without a license.

Judge Diane Lepley directed the defendant to stand as the Senator's entourage visibly braced themselves for

71

a verdict they would remember.

"By the authority vested in me by the laws of the District of Columbia," Judge Lepley declared, "I can sentence you to the maximum term of one year for DUI, five years for vehicular homicide and six months for driving without a license.

"I realize that you've suffered the loss of your wife, but she would be alive today if you were not driving under the influence of alcohol. Your blood alcohol level was nearly double the maximum limit.

"I must note also that you hold a position of public trust, and are responsible to the people of the United States in ways that average citizens are not.

"I cannot, therefore, treat this matter lightly, and I therefore sentence you to six months imprisonment, and mandatory treatment at an alcohol/drug abuse clinic.

"The term of your prison sentence will run concurrently with time in treatment.

"You will complete that treatment program and return to this court prior to completing the balance of your prison term serving in the District's prison. If at that time there is reason to believe that you have overcome whatever it was that led to this tragedy, I will commute the sentence to probation equal to the time you would have served.

"And I expect you to live up to the terms of probation."

An ashen-face Sen. Hill left the courtroom, escorted to his car by Chris Murphy.

"Bob, we have just under an hour and a half to get to Reagan for the flight to Palm Springs. Everything is arranged, and I'll accompany you to Betty Ford."

Palm Springs Airport is a pleasant regional airport with signs coated in brown paint that matches the surrounding terrain. Possibly designed by dress designers more interested in color coordination than coordination of traffic, the airport is difficult to navigate if you're driving from or into it for the first time.

As Sen. Hill walked from the Palm Springs terminal to "Avis preferred" after picking up his bags from the baggage area, the light and heat of the desert sun hit him.

Momentarily blinded by the sun and adjusting to the desert heat, he and Chris Murphy entered a late model Cadillac parked on the lot adjacent to a rear entrance to the terminal. The engine was running, air conditioning turned "on," and a Wall Street Journal lay on the front seat.

A headline on the front page of the Wall Street

Journal read:

"Conservative Leader in Exile" (with a line drawing facsimile of Sen. Hill's face).

"Shit!" Hill cries.

Chris Murphy asked, "What?"

Sen. Hill replied, "I said 'shit.' I'm in Palm Springs headed to Betty Ford, and the first thing I read is my obituary in the Wall Street Journal."

Chris replied, "Senator, I'm certain that the reports of your death are greatly exaggerated."

"Chris, that's the nicest damn thing I've heard since I was sentenced."

As they pulled out of the airport, Sen. Hill asked Chris to drive to Palm Desert to pick up something to wear at the clinic.

Palm Desert is an eight-minute drive to Rancho Mirage and the Betty Ford Clinic. Named after the wife of President Gerald Ford, the clinic attracts celebrities, including politicians of both parties.

Former President Ford lived in the Rancho Mirage golf community until his death in 2006. Former Vice President of the United States, Spiro Agnew, could be seen frequently on the Rancho Mirage golf course retrieving golf balls from the ponds that dot the golf course.

Sen. Hill knew about Rancho Mirage and Palm Desert from friends who visited President Ford and wanted to see Palm Desert's equivalent of Rodeo Drive.

Palm Springs is a comfortable home for the wealthy who remember Bob Hope, Fred Waring, Dinah Shore, Frank Sinatra, and other '50s celebrities. Bob Hill thought those street names would be changed in twenty-five years when those names no longer conjure up fond memories. But, for now, he thought, they have an allure suggesting good times and American prosperity.

On the drive to Palm Desert, Sen. Hill noticed that many storefronts in high-end shopping areas were vacant and made a mental note to look into the decline of wealth during the weak economy that followed the banking crisis of 2020.

If Palm Desert is struggling, most of America is struggling as well, he thought.

Sen. Hill spotted a place to park and asked Chris to pull in. Chris parked the rented Cadillac, and together they left the car for a walk down Waring Drive. Sen. Hill wasn't hungry though several restaurants offered an enticing opportunity to delay the drive to Betty Ford. Instead, on this day he was attracted to an art gallery named "Coda."

Bob Hill and Chris entered the gallery and were met by the owner, David Katz. Katz was an elderly merchant who knew who his possible customer was and directed him to his portrait that he priced at $1 million. Sen. Hill laughed and asked what is the price of this? He pointed at a life-like statue of a woman in a ball gown. About two feet high, the woman was wearing a gown in ivory and blue and her face was angelic. The price, $500, was reasonable, and Sen. Hill left the Coda Gallery with the statue grasped in two hands.

The drive to Betty Ford was uneventful, but Bob noticed that its entrance and reception were located behind a series of buildings that crowded out what may have been open space when the clinic was first constructed.

The clinic's staff person. Beverly Hutton, introduced herself to Sen. Hill and said, "I'm here to get you started on your journey to sobriety."

"Thank you, Ma'am," Sen. Hill replied, and he and Beverly walked through the clinic to the Senator's new quarters: a nicely-furnished bed-sitting room with a bed, couch, one desk, and two chairs looked out onto an interior courtyard.

"Where's the TV?" Sen. Hill asked.

Beverly replied, "We don't have TVs in Clinic

rooms, but there is a common room with a cable TV connection."

"You're kidding?" said Sen. Hill.

"No," Beverly said, "recovery isn't going to occur while watching TV alone, so the TV in the lounge down the hall is available, but access is restricted to one hour a night."

"Jesus," Sen. Hill exclaimed.

"The clinic is organized so you don't have much time for TV anyway, and events are designed to share what you've been going through with others in the clinic for treatment.

"Clinic psychologists will explain," Beverly continued, "that there are a number of explanations for dependency on drugs and alcohol. At some point, those who use uploads, tranquilizers, pain killers, cocaine, heroin, or alcohol become dependent on their use. In order to become users, they must be available.

"Alcohol is readily available, and use of alcohol is culturally accepted. Some cultures serve alcohol with meals. Wine is common in Latin Europe—Italy, France, Spain—and beer and hard liquor are common in northern Europe. No doubt consumption habits are related to cultural ones.

"I recall," she observed, "that Hitler's putsch began

in a Munich beer hall.

"Environment and social conditions also affect alcohol consumption. Hard liquor—bourbon, rye, scotch, and gin—are prevalent in England, Scotland, Ireland, and Wales. Ireland, particularly, is identified with drinking 'hard' liquor, as is Wales. In nineteenth-century England, consumption of gin was epidemic and a major health concern."

This recital caused Sen. Hill to recall what Alexis de Tocqueville observed in 1830: that Americans were solitary, hard liquor drinkers.

Alcohol use, he knew, affects users differently. Alcohol affects American Indians and non-Europeans from places where alcohol was not produced more immediately than persons in or from countries where alcohol production historically came later.

Significantly, Bob Hill's father was part Indian. But alcoholism wasn't the only addiction that his new colleagues at Betty Ford brought to discussions. Nor was there a consistent age of clinic "guests."

Some were college students, others middle-aged, more women than men by about 5%, some from farms and rural areas where meth amphetamines were manu-factured. But most hailed from cities and suburbs of cities and depended on dealers for their drugs.

Bob's day was organized and unchanging.

Breakfast was served at 8:00 am.

Sessions with his psychologist began at 9:00 and lasted two hours.

At 11:00, he was required to return to his room and exactly at Noon he was expected to come to lunch.

After lunch at 1:00, he attended his first group session.

These were attended by ten to fifteen patients and lasted two hours.

After those sessions, beginning at 4:00, he could use the exercise equipment that consisted of a treadmill and weights, or he could return to his room for a nap.

At 4:45, he had another group session lasting one hour, after which he went to dinner.

Meals were served in small-sized dinettes with seating for between five to ten patients assigned to each dining area.

After a dinner meal, patients were permitted to visit a reading room or a TV area, and at 7:00 they were expected to meet in a larger conference area.

Like a meeting of Alcoholics Anonymous, the 7:00 pm conference was an opportunity for patients who were within one month of leaving the clinic to talk about their addiction, or patients in their second month to talk about their treatment.

"My name is X, and I'm an addict" was the introduction that each was expected to state, adding only what form of addiction required treatment.

Bob enjoyed these public meetings, but not the morning sessions with his psychologist.

As far as Bob Hill was concerned, psychology was 98% bullshit and 2% bedside manners. If he had a drinking problem, he wasn't going to learn much from talking to Dr. Roger Core.

Dr. Core was a clinical psychologist and a member of the American Psychiatric Association that during the Cold War refused to take a stand against the psychiatric abuse of dissidents imprisoned in the Soviet Union's Gulag.

Dr. Core was prematurely bald and, apparently, proud of it because it gave him an opportunity to avoid barbers.

From a child he was certain that his barber was a Mafioso and worried that someday his time would be up.

That was a childish fear which he overcame by eating Italian food and visiting Italy.

He particularly liked Milan because the Italians didn't look Italian.

The short ones were from southern Italy, and the Milanese were tall and probably centuries ago emigrated from Germany.

Dr. Core carried a lot of other baggage for which he sought treatment by weekly visits to his psychiatrist.

Perhaps Bob Hill sensed this and was wary when Dr. Core began to probe by asking him personal questions about inadequacy, the risk of losing an election, his relationship with Mary.

That particularly upset Sen. Hill since his inattention to the road led to his wife's death. He compensated by concluding that if he had a serious drinking problem he would be looking for a drink right now.

In fact, Bob couldn't remember if he ever had a drink before lunch. Much depended on his schedule, what he had to do and whether it was okay to have a snort or wait. Most of the time he waited, but he knew that he was thinking about that drink.

That was something he could deal with, but dealing with Dr. Core was another matter.

Roger Core was a behavioral psychologist, which Bob Hill knew from his undergraduate education at Harvard meant that he reduced his science to "behaviors."

There was something limited about that approach,

Bob thought, since he was a successful politician because he discerned how people act.

People are rational and act rationally, and they may "behave," but their most important beliefs were not rooted in behavior.

You can train rats, dogs, and horses, but human beings need motivation, ideas, loves, hates, a plenitude of historical events that frame their actions.

What Dr. Core wanted to know was irrelevant, as far as Bob was concerned.

That was why he asked Beverly Hutton if the clinic had a Catholic priest who visited, or if he could leave the clinic to attend Mass. Bob Hill knew that only the Grace of God would enable him to survive "treatment" at Betty Ford and recovery from dependence on alcohol. Bob now realized that when you can see only darkness, you're alone and lost everything you love, only the Sacraments and priests who administer them can enable the return of light.

Betty was a bit shocked since most of her friends, and her patients, didn't go to church, and if they were patients at the clinic they were surely not going to be permitted to leave for church services.

But, she did know a priest in Palm Desert who was very well liked by his parishioners and by those who attended a Catholic parish in Vista Santa Rosa.

Fr. Peter Ford liked to say, to those who came to him for help, that he was a "Ford not a Lincoln."

He didn't think he was better than anyone else since how he became a priest was not his doing.

Fr. Ford was raised a Lutheran, and after graduating from college he became a banker, and when that frustrated him he chose to enter a Lutheran seminary.

That wasn't his calling either, so he took a course in "Mixology" and became a bartender.

That, he often said, was a real help when he decided to enter the Catholic priesthood. At age 38, Fr. Ford was what the Church called a "belated vocation," and since he hadn't gone to Catholic schools, what he knew about the Church was only that he needed the Church.

His seminary class with other "belated vocations" was like some of the cocktails he mixed: Some ex-military who had experienced the fragility of life and sought the comfort of eternity; a successful engineer at Bell Laboratories and another a mathematician with a degree from MIT. And there were a mix of young people pressured to become priests because they had acted "funny."

Not so long ago, when a son exposed himself to his male friends, or tried to kiss them, his parents took him aside and explained that he was committing a sin and needed to devote himself to God.

Sending him off the seminary was their way of coping with homosexuality, and, unfortunately for the Catholic Church, many of those troubled youngsters were ordained.

Peter Ford was there because he knew that he was called to serve God, and he had to get through "basic training" in order to enter a real seminary.

The mathematician from MIT was also called to serve the Lord, and Peter and he hit it off.

Their program was offered at Loyola University in Chicago, a Jesuit college, and classes were held in an area surrounded by neighborhood bars. Peter and the mathematician figured out that hitting a bar before curfew was the only way they were going to get through this program.

Every night they crossed the street and entered a local bar where they ordered boilermakers. This was not "social" drinking; it was drinking to kill the thought that yet another day of vocational training was in store for them.

Perhaps that experience explained why he liked tending bar.

There was something about Fr. Ford that Bob Hill

really liked, and only after hearing him serve Mass at the clinic did he understand.

Bob Hill said that Fr. Ford wasn't a "candy ass" who never lived a real life before becoming a priest. This man had seen it all and had turned to God because God beckoned him to come.

Bob Hill came to wish that he had experienced that himself.

The stories of clinic patients were always interesting and revealed what Bob discerned as a pattern of denial, the hurt and havoc that addiction inflicted on others, realization that they had a problem and, finally, treatment.

How they got into treatment was always different.

Sometimes, family members conducted interventions to persuade them to seek help. Others, like Bob, went into treatment—or jail.

At the start, Bob Hill wasn't prepared to admit he was an alcoholic.

"Sure," he said to himself, "I drink. But I can stop any time I want."

During the first several weeks of his stay, he really missed not having a drink.

"Boy," he said after one of his first group meetings, "what I'd give for ten minutes at my office."

He knew his interest in going to the office wasn't to read his mail.

Nights, however, were the worst.

Before entering the clinic, Bob used alcohol to get through the day and to put himself to sleep at night. Now without a nighttime drink, he found it difficult to sleep.

He awakened frequently and went back to sleep only with difficulty.

He tried to read as a way to put himself to sleep, but that too was difficult. At some point in the night he simply had to get some sleep, but the feeling of sleepiness often didn't kick in until 3:30 am.

Bob's addiction was wearing him down and he knew it.

His quarters were comfortable enough.

A twin bed on one side faced a desk, chair, and book shelf across from his bed.

On the left side of the room there was a sofa and coffee table.

Those few furnishings filled up the small living area with a small room for a shower and toilet and a closet for clothing.

On the bookshelf, Bob placed the statue he purchased at Coda gallery.

The elegant porcelain lady was formally dressed and looked down on the bedroom area as if waiting for Bob to get dressed for an evening out.

There are no "evenings out" when you're in treatment, so she would have to wait until Bob's treatment ended, and he could take her to his home on Capitol Hill.

Boy did Bob wish he was home.

8.

"Tonight, No Light will Shine on Me"

Bob Hill preferred Dolly Parton to Bob Dylan, but a line from one of Dylan's songs came to mind during his first week at Betty Ford.

"One more night, I will wait for the light
While the wind blows high above the tree
Oh, I miss my darling so
I didn't mean to see her go
But tonight no light will shine on me."

The death of Mary Hill was a terrible blow that, were he not confined at the Betty Ford Clinic in Palm Springs, Sen. Hill would have sought recovery in booze.

Days at Betty Ford were filled with activities, but nights were difficult.

Bob had always been a fitful sleeper, waking up at 3:00 am most nights, and trying to get back to sleep.

He tried everything from prayer, to watching TV, to checking his e-mail, but for two hours between 3:00 and 5:00, he couldn't get back to sleep. By the time he entered the clinic, this sleeping pattern was ingrained and, sure enough, he'd fall asleep at 10 pm and awaken at 3:00 am.

There wasn't a TV in his room that he could turn to, and he tried reading, but that merely caused him to stay awake.

One night, about the third week, he awakened at 3 am and felt the presence of someone else in the room. He knew that was his imagination since no one could enter the clinic without causing the alarms to sound. He looked around the room and up at the bookshelf where he placed that porcelain statue.

He could have sworn that one eye of that figure had winked.

Now Bob understood that he was in trouble. All those drinks probably impaired his mind and his imagination was keeping him awake and animating lifeless objects. Finally, he realized that he needed counseling.

But, how do you explain that a figurine is communicating with you.

If that bit of personal information got out of the

building, he really would be dead politically!

So, Bob did what he had learned to do as a boy trying to avoid confrontation with his father.

He avoided thinking about what disturbed him.

Unfortunately, a few nights later he awakened, again sensing that someone was in his room, maybe not a person, but a spirit.

Was it his conscience, perhaps?

Looking up, the statue of a lady in a blue gown blinked at him again.

"What in the hell is going on," he asked himself.

He wasn't imagining this.

"It" was real.

What do you do when you experience something that is paranormal?

But this experience wasn't just in Bob's mind, he actually saw what he saw. There was something there, in his room, and it was telling him something.

Finally, one night as 3:00 am approached, Bob sensed again that there was someone in his room. Startled, he awakened to see the form of a woman standing by his bedside. It was the statue, come to life and waiting.

"What in the hell is going on?" he shouted.

The figure looked at him and held out her hand.

Bob reached out and touched her hand.

She tightened her grip and pulled him up. He was now standing beside a woman who began to dance.

Suddenly the clinics alarms sounded and he looked toward the door. A patient had opened a door to a garden. The sound had startled him, and when he turned back, the figure was gone.

9.

Fr. Peter Ford

Bob Hill was in trouble, and he knew it. His future political career was shattered by the death of his wife in an accident when he was driving under the influence.

He was hallucinating about a dancing woman's statue that came to life in his clinic room at night, and the protective shield he created to keep his private life separate from the public life as a politician didn't work for him in treatment.

Morning group discussion sessions with other patients were the hardest.

As a Catholic, Bob Hill knew about right and wrong from Catholic school. Even at Harvard, he was attracted to a course on Aristotle who taught about "right by nature," man's ability to act and the moral dimension of action, and Aristotle's discussion about the best constitution.

So, instinctively, the psychologist Roger Core

raised his hackles. Dr. Core was a behaviorist, a type of modern science that examines social and personal life in quantitative terms that can be measured. Man's "behaviors" can be predicted based on "inputs" and "outputs" and "systems" of behavior. Alcohol dependency from that perspective, was a behavior, not a moral failure.

Coming to understand his behavior was the goal of group discussions. Bob regretted those meetings because patients were expected to state aspects of their personal lives that his career shielded from public scrutiny.

Bob needed to talk to someone, but who could he trust? Fr. Peter Ford, a priest at Saint Augustine Church in Palm Desert, was well known in the "Springs." His parish was not a "normal" Catholic parish because his parishioners were successful, well-off, and not burdened by life's monetary issues.

Many were homosexuals who had hidden their sexuality throughout their ordinary lives and in retirement had "come out."

Others had moved to the Springs to live with their lovers after divorcing their wives of forty years.

Some were successful businessmen for whom golf was more than recreation—it was religion.

There were "normal," hardworking blue collar workers, mostly Hispanic who commuted to work in the Springs from nearby Hispanic communities. They attended the 6:00 am Mass before work, struggled with English, and lived for their children.

The best thing about Saint Augustine Church was Fr. Peter Ford.

The 21st century is a time of sacral turmoil in the Catholic Church. What once constituted "orthodoxy" was no longer certain. The days of G. K. Chesterton ("My doxy is orthodoxy") and Cardinal John Henry Newman were long gone.

Newman had died in 1890, a year before Pope Leo XIII issued his encyclical, *Rerum Novarum*. And Chesterton died five years after the encyclical *Quadragesimo anno* of Pope Pius XI that unintentionally eclipsed the teaching of St. Thomas Aquinas with a doctrine of "Social Justice."

Chesterton is remembered by the Chesterton Society for concern about "social injustice, the culture of death, statism, assaults on religion, and attacks on the family and on the dignity of the human person."

Chesterton and Hilaire Belloc addressed economics from a Catholic perspective that they called "distributism." Classical liberalism was rooted in the ideas of

Adam Smith, Jean-Baptiste Say, and David Ricardo and the British empiricist tradition.

For Chesterton, ideas were more than the impressions of "bodies in motion." There are "innate ideas" that we experience before we are born which are impressed on the human "soul." Reason can discover absolutes, truth itself, and "natural law." And he understood that natural law was distinguishable from the "law of nature" of Thomas Hobbes and John Locke.

This discussion by orthodox Catholics which followed Pope Leo XIII's *Rerum Novarum* interested Fr. Ford.

Rerum Novarum challenged a dominant "liberal" ideology of freedom, contracts, labor, and market value. At bottom, the value of labor was not something that could be established by markets alone. Labor sustains human life, and a good society protects the laborer in order to assure his survival and salvation.

All that was to the good, but Chesterton could sense in his bones the trend toward "statism" that had yet to become full blown by 1890.

Fr. Ford was a 21st century Catholic priest in the American church, but how he got there, where he came from, and what he aspired to achieve were uncommon.

The Catholic Church has a problem. All aspects of

American culture tend away from the foundations of "Catholicism." That very word was not attractive to Fr. Ford. For him, being Catholic meant to do—to live— as Christ wanted us to live. You could systematize that teaching into an "ism," but in doing so you lost the central character of faith found in love, life, community, and service.

"God so loved the world that he gave his only begotten son," were words from John, Chapter 3, verse 16, that opened up the soul of man to God's love. Even before the birth of Jesus, God created the world out of nothing—*ex nihilo*.

That mystery intrigued Fr. Ford.

Why would an omnipotent God, self-sufficient unto Himself, want to create a world for man to in-habit?

That act had something to do with His sense of humor, a love for company and the response of mortal beings to the author of Being. God wants man to work out his salvation and created a habitat, placed in a favorable orbit around the sun, where that was made possible.

That, of course, was a dividing line between Protes-tants and Catholics.

Protestants believe that man is saved by grace, not

works. The key to eternal life is belief. Works will follow from that belief, but works do not impact the promise of salvation to all those who believe.

Born and raised by a Protestant working class family of English descent, Fr. Ford believed what he was taught and nourished his hopes for eternal life.

Normal life intervened, however, as when he stole a piece of candy from the local grocer. As he matured, he was attracted to women and had a brief affair when he was nineteen with a neighbor.

She was his age and her parents left for a weekend, and she invited him to "come by." One thing led to another and she gave him oral sex, and he experienced an orgasm. Penetration didn't occur, but every experience that comes with sexual intercourse was present. Afterward, he felt shame and wondered if there was anything he could do to wash away that feeling. Believing that he was "saved" didn't do it.

At college, Peter Ford studied History. Of course, that was crazy for someone from a working class family. Economics or Business were the ticket to improving one's lot. But the human story interested him and especially the story of America.

Names like DeSoto, Columbus, Cabot, Ponce de León, Balboa, and Verrazano excited his interest and when others were chasing coeds, Peter Ford could be found in the library reading about these explorers.

After graduation in 1985, he found the book by Daniel Boorstin titled *The Discoverers: A History of Man's Search to Know His World and Himself.* He had been working in a bank for two years, but quit, kicked around, and took a course in "mixology." He became very good making mixed drinks with fruit and as a bartender had a clientele of women who wanted to be seen, have a drink, but not get drunk.

As a bartender he learned about the glories and pains of his customers and brought his good common sense to discussions that attracted even more customers who sought his company. By 1989, when he was twenty-five years old, he decided to pursue ordination in the Anglican Church. He was admitted to the Anglican seminary in Berkeley, California, the Church Divinity School of the Pacific. There for three years he pursued the Master of Divinity (M.Div.) Degree.

His love of reading and the sociality he developed as a bartender helped get him through a rigorous course of study leading to the Masters of Divinity.

His studies included two courses in History. The first covered the history of Christianity from its origins to the late medieval period.

The second covered the development of Protestant Christianity as a world movement from the fifteenth to the late twentieth century.

He studied "Theology" that introduced him to systematic theology and such topics as God, creation, Trinity, Christology, theological anthropology, sin and salvation, grace, and pneumatology. A second course in Theology focused on the sacraments, eschatology, and hermeneutics.

The study of Ethics dealt with Christian ethics, its history of theoretical foundations.

Liturgics and Music taught the history and theology of past liturgical experience and sacramental theology, with special attention to the Book of Common Prayer.

He also took a course in church music. The Anglican worship service can range from guitar to symphonic music, and Peter was definitely in the "High Church" school when it came to music.

He concluded his studies with a course on the art of preaching, exegesis of scripture, sermon design and presentation. He needed some training in that area since he was not a "preacher." Peter Ford was a communicator and specialized in personal communication. When you were with Fr. Ford, you felt that he was with you in spirit.

Perhaps for that reason, he really liked weekly "Community Nights" where the school community met for a catered dinner—following a 5:30 Eucharist service—to talk, listen to a lecture, and get to know one another.

That "sodality" was the high point of his week, and his company at dinner was sought by his fellow students.

Upon ordination in 1992, he became a priest in the Anglican parish of Christ the King in San Jose, California. He was now 28 years old and was assigned to the "Youth Ministry."

In his heart, Peter Ford was an old man. Little of the modern world attracted him—not Rock music, sports, motion pictures, or fast cars. He drove an old two-door Chevy and enjoyed driving some parishioners who didn't have cars to the grocery or their doctors.

That, too, was an opportunity to hone his social skills and to learn about aspects of daily life that he missed when growing up. He learned about the aches and pains of his parishioners, their children, illnesses and aspirations for their families.

Still, by the time he was 36 years old, he felt that something was missing. He felt the need to justify his existence, to do something to earn his salvation.

Beginning in the 1970s, the Anglican Church in America, officially The Protestant Episcopal Church of the U.S.A., went through a bruising battle between traditionalists and modernists. Their battleground was the 1928 Book of Common Prayer (BCP) vs. an alternative version. The Society for the Preservation of the Book of Common Prayer worked to save the original BCP from deconstructionists who turned their attention to women's ordination, ordination of homosexuals, and blessings for same sex unions.

Those "reforms" were accomplished in the late 1970s, and though Peter Ford became an Anglican priest twenty years later, he found himself uncomfortable with women priests. He had friends who were homosexual—who didn't?—but their ordination was too much.

He decided that the Catholic Church would be a better "home."

Becoming a Catholic priest at his age was considered a "belated vocation," and Catholic Bishops were not quick to admit to seminary older men. They preferred to cultivate Catholics to become priests in high school and admit them to seminary after completing college. When Peter Ford sought admission to a Catholic seminary in San Diego, his Bishop denied his request.

That was not uncommon. Bishops in the Catholic Church are more celebrated for their business ability and, especially, their ability to build physical churches. Contemporary wags refer to this as the Bishops' "erection complex."

People, not buildings, interested Peter Ford, but he saw that the course taken by the Episcopal Church was dividing Christians in ways that would make recovery from the divisions in Christianity impossible.

Faced with his Bishop's decision to deny him access to St. Patrick's Seminary in Menlo Park, he sought admission to Mundelein Seminary in Chicago. Nearby Loyola University of Chicago had a one semester "prep" program for "Belated Vocations," and Peter Ford enrolled. There he was in a group of fifteen adults ranging in age from 24 to 42. There was a Franciscan brother, an engineer from Bell Labs, a Mathematician from MIT, a hair stylist, a 25-year-old "Trust Baby" from a wealthy New York family, a former enlisted soldier who had served four years in the U.S. military, a graduate student at Notre Dame and Fr. Peter Ford.

The purpose of the program was to screen and qualify candidates from the priesthood and, in the case of the program's director, to block from the priesthood males of confused sexuality. The Hair Stylist was the first to go, offended with the Director of the program who insisted on calling him "sweetie." It became apparent to Fr. Ford that good Catholic families whose sons revealed questionable sexual interests worked to persuade them to seek salvation by committing themselves to the celibate life of a Catholic priest. The Trust Baby liked to kiss boys, and that demanded swift action from his parents. The others were normal males who discovered that they had a religious vocation. They had made a choice to become Catholic priests and were serious about that commitment.

Strangely, these were exactly the kind of men who would be excellent priests, but their Bishops wanted younger, more malleable, adolescents they could shape in their own mold. Despite that, four of these men with belated vocations were admitted to seminary. The mathematician, a former student at Brooklyn Poly, was problematic. He was raised in the Russian Orthodox faith, spoke fluent Russian, and was simply too complicated a case. He was denied admission to St. Joseph's Seminary at Dunwoodie in Yonkers, NY.

Fr. Ford learned ten years later that he died of cardiac arrest on August 15, the Feast of the Assumption of the Blessed Mary Virgin. "Poetic justice," Fr. Ford said to himself as he said Mass the next morning.

Even with as much seminary training as he had as an Anglican, Fr. Ford found that his studies at Dunwoodie opened up a world that was neglected in his earlier training.

He started with a seminar on the theological vision of Joseph Ratzinger (Pope Benedict XVI), whose career as a Cardinal featured the defense of orthodoxy.

In a course titled "Catholic Renaissance Humanism," he read St. Thomas More's *Utopia* and various works of More written while incarcerated in the Tower as well as St. John Fisher's Exposition on the Penitential Psalms and his essay on St. Mary Magdalene.

Martyrdom was a present reality in those days, and the good father who taught the course wanted it known, that in our day, too, Catholic priests experience a form of martyrdom.

Another titled "Theology and Catholic Literature" studied literary criticism and theological interpretation of short stories, poetry, and novels with a Catholic perspective by writers such as Flannery O'Connor and Gerard Manley Hopkins. According to the course description, this gave seminarians "the opportunity to see how Catholic doctrines of creation, faith, conversion, and redemption reveal their depths in the joys, sorrows, and pathos of human lives."

A course titled "Hebrews and Revelation" studied the theology of the letter to the Hebrews and the Book of Revelation. That gave him a sense of the apocalyptic derived from ancient Israel and the early Church.

"Now, this is exciting stuff," Peter Ford said to himself, and he sailed through his M.Div. program at Dunwoodie and was ordained a priest in the Brooklyn Diocese. By the time he completed his studies, he might have been criticized for being "overeducated."

But his love of the lives of "ordinary" people had grounded him.

By the time he arrived at St. Augustine Church in Palm Desert, Fr. Peter Ford was a gift of God to the patients at Betty Ford. He said Mass on Saturdays at the clinic and made himself available for consultations with patients who simply wanted to talk.

Sen. Bob Hill was one of them.

"Father," he said, "I've got a problem."

The "problem" was nothing like anything that Fr. Ford had encountered before.

He understood all the sins that men and women are prone to commit, but none had come to him with a tale about a statue that became alive—at night. There are histories of "visions" of Christ, the Virgin Mary, and the Apostles of Christ.

But, a non-religious statue of a woman wearing a ball gown? That didn't fit the mold.

What was going on?

Fr. Ford asked himself, and carefully questioned Sen. Hill to learn as much about his experience as he could understand. Sen. Hill likened it to the scene in *The Terminator* when Sarah Conner is analyzed by a psychiatrist and understands what will happen to her if she tells him that a robot from the future has come back in time to kill her.

Sen. Hill's political career was already in shambles. Add to that this stuff about a living statue, and everything he valued in his political life would be destroyed. Fr. Ford understood that, of course, and imagined that even without this scandal, the likelihood of Sen. Hill's re-election was not high.

Confronted with a deeply troubled man, he asked for as much information as his patient would divulge. It became clear that Sen. Hill was not experiencing a vision; he was encountering a living presence. He remembered that on one or two occasions while sleeping he became aware of a presence in his room. He attributed that experience to something in his subconscious self that was awakened when he slept.

But a dancing woman was, clearly, not a part of Sen. Hill's persona. This was something exterior to himself. But what could that being be if not a hallucination?

Sen. Hill had been a steady drinker, but he hadn't had a drink since his accident. He wasn't given medications by the Clinic staff, so the external source of this experience must be not of this world. But where?

Fr. Ford's discussions with Sen. Hill lasted half an hour each day, three times a week over fourteen weeks. During that time he learned that he came from Eastern Pennsylvania, went to Harvard, ran for election to the U.S. House of Representatives as a Republican from Allentown, once a steel town, and now within commuting distance of New York, a place for mid-executives trying to avoid housing costs in New York City, and that he was deeply "pro-life."

The incumbent Republican Senator from Pennsylvania he defeated was "pro-choice." Sen. Hill mixed his social conservatism with a commitment to free market economics and lowering of taxes. As a Catholic, he appealed across Party lines to "Reagan Democrats" and was elected to the United States Senate on his second attempt.

His late wife, Mary, he learned, was "more Catholic

than the Pope," and resisted her anger at her husband's drinking through prayer and charity work.

Bob Hill told him that she recited the Rosary fifty times a day.

That datum was important, Fr. Ford thought. The "Para-Normal" is simply defined as not explainable by the scientific method. Fr. Ford didn't like that word nor the word "supernatural." God is not "above" but "in" all things and can be known by use of human reason--not blind faith.

So, if what Bob Hill was experiencing was real, it wasn't supernatural but in reality at a level that the Senator experienced.

Fr. Ford began to suspect a connection between the Senator's late wife, Mary, and the statue of a woman in a ball gown. That line of reasoning had potential, but not something that Sen. Hill could discuss with the Clinic's resident psychologist, Roger Core. To add to Sen. Hill's dilemma, he began to refer to Dr. Core as "Rotten Core."

The world of modern behavioral psychologists is a world of secure assumptions and what Sen. Hill thought was an unreasonable faith in science.

First of all, Sen. Hill remembered from his study of Aristotle that reason, the basis of science (knowledge), is not mere ratiocination.

Man's calculative ability is overarched by a higher reason that enables man to discern true reality. That includes reality that we do not experience from our senses. We perceive that reality in our mind which is an aspect of our souls.

So, if Sen. Hill was going to pass muster with this modern Guardian of empirical knowledge, he would have to speak his language. He would work from Fr. Ford's assumption that his experience of the dancing woman originated from his late wife, but he would tell "Rotten Core" that he wasn't sleeping well.

From that he knew that Dr. Core would explore a range of empirical causes from possible latent injuries from his accident, inadequacy in loss of support of his late wife, or the long-term effects of heavy drinking. All three explanations made sense to Dr. Core and Sen. Hill admitted that he had experienced a slight concussion from the accident, and that, yes, he depended on his wife, and she was no longer alive. But, most important, someone who depended on alcohol to go to sleep will experience sleeplessness in its absence.

With that little lie, Sen. Hill could be assured that Dr. Core would report that his addiction had been overcome and that with a commitment to attending

Alcoholics Anonymous meetings, he could expect to avoid a reversal.

10.

Return

Finally, the day of his release came, Chris Murphy arrived to travel back to Washington with him, and he collected his things, packed his suitcase, and walked out of the clinic. As he stepped outside, the sun blinded him, and he slipped. The figurine that he was carrying slipped from his hand and shattered into three pieces on the sidewalk.

Bob was more than upset, but he didn't let Chris know that this was a shattering event for him, too. He slowly bent down, gently picked up the pieces and placed them in his suitcase.

His first day back in his office at Hart Senate Office Building his staff greeted him with delight, and he began to return to the day-to-day routine of a United States Senator. His office bar was gone, and the little refrigerator where he kept vodka cold now contained bottles of Ensure.

Monday mornings were spent reviewing his schedule for the week, and this Monday his staff pointed out that Mary Hill had arranged for the two of them to attend a Viennese Waltz organized by Congressional staff. This year's event was at the Organization of States building, and he was expected to attend. The marble face of the building, located about a five-minute walk from the White House, is especially bright when illuminated at night.

Bob had nothing else to do that Saturday, so he put on his tuxedo, which now fit quite well since he had lost twenty pounds by not drinking, and he, Chris Murphy and Chris's wife, set off for an evening of Viennese waltzes.

The Organization of American States building is a gorgeous structure built to house the organization of thirty countries of the Americas and the Caribbean. Large private events can accommodate hundreds of revelers, full orchestras, and bands, and this evening the organizers went all out with foods, pastries, fruits, and edibles to delight most gourmands.

Sen. Hill could hear the first strains of the Blue Danube as he entered the main hall. There were at least one hundred couples dancing a waltz. The women's gowns floated as they moved and the men in tuxedos moved with them. Some had obviously practiced and gracefully moved across the ballroom floor. Others clomped along, but all seemed to be enjoying themselves.

Bob too began to get into the mood when he felt the presence of someone to his right. It was the woman who had visited him at night in the clinic. "Hello, Senator," she said, "I'm Apollonia."

11.

Recovery

Settling down to his duties in the United States Senate in 2018 wasn't as easy as Bob Hill thought it would be. The stigma of drunk driving, a judgment of manslaughter, and mandatory recovery at Betty Ford was with him every minute of every day. Only the statutory two years remaining in his six-year term of office as a United States Senator assured that, each morning, he had a place to go.

But, Bob Hill was troubled not only by loss of Mary, but loss of his Presidential ambitions. He felt in his bones that his understanding of American National Security and Foreign Policy was much needed, especially after the "imperial" foreign policies of the George W. Bush Administration destroyed the GOP 'brand' of limited government.

Leaving the Mayflower Hotel that day, Bob Hill expected to run for President in 2024. Now he would be lucky to be re-elected to the U.S. Senate in 2020.

His home in Allentown had been sold to pay for attorneys, and after paying off personal credit card debts, Sen. Bob Hill lived from paycheck to paycheck. Not that he had to scrounge to pay the electricity; annual salary for a U.S. Senator at $174,000 gave him a comfortable monthly "take-home" even after federal income taxes of $33,000. But, Bob Hill lived in DC where after federal taxes and withholding for Social Security his annual net income dropped to $117,000.

Most Americans would be delighted to live on $10,000 a month, but the demands of Bob's job as a United State Senator left him with little at the end of each month.

Bob Hill was now faced with a very major career choice: stay in office and seek reelection or retire at the end of his term in 2020. At 45, retirement from politics as a washed-up former Senator wasn't an attractive option. Deciding to stay the course, he said to himself, "I'll have to bull through this shit."

The Presidential election of 2024 was five year's off, and Sen. George O Walker was planning to run for President. President Donald Trump was expected to win re-election in 2020 making the presidential election in 2024 a contest for an "open seat."

In 2024, Senator Walker would be 75, if his health held up. Bob Hill would be 51 in 2024.

Maybe, just maybe, Bob thought, voters would forget or forgive him, and he could achieve his long term ambition to become President of the United States.

That was how Bob Hill "framed" his political ambitions: re-election in 2020 and a run for President in 2024.

Hatred is a major motive in American politics, but for Bob Hill, hatred of George Walker was personal. First of all, Walker was fat. How a rotund politician could win a race for Mayor of Dayton explained why Ohio, was, as Bob put it, "fucking dumb." Going as far back to Gov. John Kasich, Bob Hill believed Ohio was a place where losers with no hard edges won elections.

What was it about Ohio, Bob asked himself.

This really bothered him, so he went to the trouble of calling a college friend from Cincinnati who shared Bob's political views.

His buddy, Chris O'Day, wore his ethnicity on his sleeve, green ties and his affinity for red heads. Something about "red-headed broads," as Chris described them. And Chris would know: he had married two, divorced one and had three red-headed children.

Over drinks at The Palm on 19th Street NW in Washington, DC, Chris and Bob ordered New York strip steaks, and Chris had an Absolute Martini, "up." Bob chose Perrier. The back room of the Palm is frequented by DC "Think Tank" denizens, DNC politicians, and wealthy lobbyists.

The Palm was founded in 1920 in Manhattan near the 45th Street headquarters of the Hearst organization's New York Daily Mirror. The Daily Mirror closed in 1963, but The Palm in New York expanded and opened in Washington, DC, where politicians, media personalities and other members of the powers in our nation's Capital City chose to dine on steaks and lobster and, most importantly, be seen.

Chris was in town to do some lobbying on behalf of a new Wal-Mart outlet that needed an "off ramp" off I-75. But, with Bob, the talk was about red-heads and Ohio's politics.

"Why," Bob asked, "does Ohio elect plain vanilla goo-goos?"

Chris had asked himself that, too, since he had done some national campaigns for conservative politicians, none from Ohio, however.

"Ohio," Chris said, "never had a Conservative movement. Only one Congressman, Buz Lukens, tried to buck the system, promised to vote 'No,' and ended up in prison for taking bribes.

"Think of Barry Goldwater and Ronald Reagan," Chris said, "none was from Ohio. But that was the 1960s and 70s. You had to go back to the 1950s and Bob Taft, three quarters of a century ago, to find a Conservative Republican from Ohio.

"Sure, there was Jim Jordan from Ohio's 4th," Bob said, "but Jordan lives in a rural area and has the seasonal vision of a farmer on a small farm."

Lima (as in "leen"), Ohio, wasn't all that far from Pittsburgh's four excellent universities, but Jordan studied Economics at Wisconsin where he became a champion wrestler, then earned the MA in education from Ohio state.

Not satisfied, he went on to earn a law degree from Capital University in Columbus.

Still, even though he was "over educated," like an earthworm, Jim Jordan lacked ambition and stuck to the ways of the small farmers in central Ohio. Jordan wasn't going anywhere, Bob Hill and George Walker agreed. Plus Bob observed, "I didn't like Denny Hastert, another fucking wrestler."

Denny Hastert succeeded Newt Gingrich as Speaker of the House. Much later it was learned the

Hastert had molested young boys at the high school where he was a wrestling coach.

Bob Hill was a "big picture" politician and had trouble talking to constituents about "off ramps," pharmaceutical prices and teenage suicide. He was interested in what the People's Republic of China would do, if we gave defensive weapons to Taiwan, and increased transfer of missiles to South Korea and Japan, and he couldn't sleep some nights worrying about the Iranians.

"That fucking Jimmy Carter blew it when the rag heads seized the American Embassy in Tehran," Bob observed. "So we lose fifty-two embassy employees, but we save America from nukes lobbed at New York by the Mullahs!"

Bob may not become President, but he thought like one.

That's why Bob hated the Republican Senator from Ohio—he thought like a local politician, plus he was a fat meatball!

But, Bob had more important things on his mind.

12.

Dr. Apollonia McCarthy

Despite his many problems: a wife killed, a political career destroyed, and a Presidential election looming in which Bob Hill was, at best a "spoiler," was not "good." But all was not gloom and doom in the life of Sen. Bob Hill.

There was that woman in a blue ball gown that visited him at night in his room at Betty Ford.

Bob concluded that this encounter was "mystic," not a word often used by politicians. But, when he was at Harvard he enrolled in a religious studies course on mystics. His choice was strictly by chance. A course on Congress was cancelled when the professor died in the arms of one of his students, and this one on mystics was undersubscribed. Maybe, he thought, that's because this was Harvard, not someplace down South where "religion" is a way of life.

That's the one thing about home in Allentown that

he missed, the presence of believers. That helped him understand that the experience of a woman in a ball gown was a gift from God. He might have felt special for that, but his "mystics" course taught him that everyone has mystic experiences. We interpret them differently, but we all have them.

The difficulty he had with this "gift" was that he asked "Why." That was Fr. Ford's mistake, too. He tried to figure out why Bob was having these visions and traced them to Bob's late wife Mary. The connection seemed obvious, but if we assume a deceased partner is active in this world that can't explain anything other than what we "assume."

But, if Fr. Ford had asked Bob what he experienced, its looks, the way it felt, or if "it" made any sound, he might have had a better understanding.

Bob likened it to what he learned in that course about mystics. They, the mystics, experienced something variously called a "revelation," "other-worldly," supernatural, or a 'turning around."

"That jived," Bob said to himself, "with that reading in another course I took at Harvard, and Plato's allegory of 'the cave.' In his *Republic*, Plato explained that we are "compelled to turn around."

That's pretty definitive, Bob thought. "I'm not

making this up. "She, the lady in the blue ball gown, is real."

The "chance" meeting of her actual person at that Viennese ball wasn't an accident. Apollonia came to the ball looking for Bob. Her best friend, Bob's wife, invited her months before, and this was her way of honoring her friend from Swissvale.

For Bob, of course, realizing that he and Apollonia were "connected" in a mystical way erased his personal cares and lit a way in his mind to forgiveness and peace.

"Peace," he said to himself, "I may now be in peace." But, as when he had to tell Fr. Ford about that lady who visits him in his room at Betty Ford, what in the hell was he going to say to Apollonia? "Hi, we met at the clinic" or "Gee, I like your blue gown."

Besides that, Apollonia was a real "looker."

Here was a gorgeous woman to whom he was immediately attracted on a spiritual and physical basis, but the spirit that connected them was known only to Bob Hill.

That didn't stop him.

He had to know more about her, her connection to Mary, where she grew up, why she had not married, and her medical practice.

Bob Hill had strained his neck in that fatal accident,

and though it hadn't bothered him in more than a year, he asked his Chief of Staff, Chris Murphy, to call Apollonia's office and ask for an appointment.

The "Family Clinic" occupied the first floor of an office building in Old Town, Alexandria. Bob and Mary would go to Old Town for dinner at Landini Brothers, an Italian restaurant that had a terrific Pomodoro pasta dish. One of Bob's biggest donors, founder of a large Pittsburgh corporation, would go there for lunch with Bob when he was in DC and, like Bob before his clinic days, would drink two or three vodka martinis.

He later died from drink, but not before making a large donation to Bob's campaign for re-election to the Senate.

Bob now had a plan. He'd go to the clinic for therapy and invite Apollonia to Landini's.

Dr. Apollonia McCarthy had never married. Her career as a physician and care for her elderly parents occupied her life. Raised in the Eastern Orthodox Church, she welcomed the celebration of "fixed" feasts and especially the "moveable" feasts of Pascha (Easter)—the beginning of Great Lent, Ascension, and Pentecost. And like her friend, Mary Hill, for whom the Rosary was a source of strength, she would recite the Eastern Orthodox eighth-century "Jesus Prayer" multiple times a day.

"O Lord, Jesus Christ, Son of God, have mercy upon me, a sinner."

Apollonia was an only child and felt responsible for the care of her mother and father. Braddock, Pennsylvania, where she grew up had declined since she was in college, and she moved her parents to a comfortable home in Pittsburgh's Oakland district, not far from Pitt. She retained a live-in assistant to prepare their meals and drive them to events that interested them. Both parents had passed away the year of Mary Hill's tragic death. She had been mourning the loss of her best friend when Bob Hill scheduled an appointment at her clinic.

Bob Hill, at age 45, was five years older than Apollonia who had kept in shape by walking and workouts at a fitness center in nearby Alexandria, Virginia, a focus of activity for upscale Virginia suburbanites and DC residents. She had a terrific grip, which Bob noticed immediately when he arrived for his clinic appointment.

"What's the problem, Senator," she asked.

Bob decided to come clean and admit that the pain he experienced from his accident was no longer a problem, but he thought she might have some sugges-

tions for staying healthy under the stressful conditions
of his political career.

He admitted that he had given up alcohol and that
had opened up new venues that he was filling up with
more work. He would arrive at his office most days at
6:00 am and leave around 8:00 pm. His bid for re-
election required weekend travel to central Pennsylvania towns and larger meetings in Philly and
Pittsburgh. His staff, he had to admit, were happy when
he left the office early on Friday for campaign travel.

"Well," Dr. McCarthy said, "I'll need to know more.
Why not discuss this over dinner some evening?"

Bob Hill's jaw dropped as he stammered his assent
to a dinner invitation.

"How about tonight at Landini's?"

13.

Timing is Everything

After the August 2018 recess, Bob had to focus on his bid for reelection to the U.S. Senate from Pennsylvania in 2020. He had sold his home in Allentown and used Chris Murphy's address in Pittsburgh as his residence. The change of residence from Eastern to Western Pennsylvania ordinarily would have made a "splash," but everyone thought that Sen. Bob Hill was washed up.

It certainly appeared that way. Though in politics appearances are important, timing is everything, and Bob felt that time was on his side.

He plotted how to get to November 2020 from August 2018—two years and three months distant. During that time, he had to change a public impression that he was washed up to being alive, well and ready for another six years.

Fortunately, his campaign manager knew how to

do that. Steve Weissman had become a pollster while
working for CBS News and shared CBS polling results
with his first client, a conservative running for the U.S.
Senate from New York.

Steve, son of a Jewish taxi driver, grew up in New
York City public housing, attended the City University
of New York, and used his mathematics ability to learn
survey research.

Always dressed in a suit with a dress shirt opened
at his collar, Steve looked out of place in the circle of
his conservative clients. More than anything, besides
his manners that marked him as a "New York Jew," as
one of his competitors caustically remarked, was
Steve's voice—clear, articulate and conveying sincerity
uncommon in politics. That made him stand out from
the crowd of other pollsters for conservative politicians.

And because he was Jewish and a political conservative, he caught the attention of conservative candidates running for office in districts with a sizeable
Jewish population. What caught Bob Hill's attention,
however, was Weissman's desire to educate Republican
donors and candidates about how far to the Left that
Jewish voters had gone. Weisman thought that Jewish
voters had gone so far Leftward that they jeopardized

Conservative support for the State of Israel.

Bob learned from Steve and modified his foreign policy views as he came to understand how the national interest of the United States is mixed with the desire of Israel to survive in an area of hate-filled neighbor countries.

Bob had barely won his first term in 2010 as a Member of the House of Representatives from Pennsylvania's District 7. He did a little better in 2012, but the 7th Congressional district was redistricted in 2014, the year before he ran for the U.S. Senate. He served two full terms in the House and established himself as a cost-cutter, an advocate of economic growth and cyber-security.

Bob took a course at Harvard from a visiting professor who held to the notion that entrepreneurs are critical to creation of jobs. They create markets, he said, by committing their sweat to ideas they believed would attract financing and customers. Entrepreneurs came in all sizes and shapes and a college degree or lack of one made no difference.

Both Steve Jobs and Bill Gates were college drop outs.

For Gates and Jobs, timing was important as they were intrigued by information technology and computer programming at the moment all the pieces for personal computers were there to make an entirely new industry. Steve Jobs and Bill Gates were focused, driven, and intelligent and willing to work hard with no guarantees of success. But Bob's instructor made it a point to say that entrepreneurs don't always succeed with their first enterprise. Many try several times before finding the one idea that fits what they know, their financial resources, and their desire to try again.

"Persistence pays" was what Bob learned from that class and understood that he could be re-elected, if he persisted.

So Bob made economic growth, lower taxes and giving citizens freedom to start their own businesses his major themes. His opponent campaigned on a platform of "jobs." "Jobs are good," Bob argued, "but I'll work to create conditions that enable you to start your own business." He didn't know that would appeal to voters in the general election, but that's what he believed.

Apparently, voters in Pennsylvania agreed, and U.S. Senator Bob Hill came to Capitol Hill in 2014.

Now he had to persuade those voters to forgive him and give him another chance. That's where Steve Weissman applied his touch to shaping Bob's public image. Candidates for office knew that Steve was different from the many political operatives selling their high-cost services to their campaigns. Steve had a warmth of personality that convinced candidates that he cared.

One candidate in Oregon, Burt Egstrom, who retained Steve's services in a race for the House of Representatives realized that after he won. A few months after taking office representing his home District from the state capital, Salem, all the way to the Idaho border, Steve showed up with some new survey results.

Wearing a suit with a white shirt and tie open at the neck, Steve paged through his survey results pointing out five areas where his candidate's views were at odds with his constituents. "Burt," Steve said, "your constituents don't like you. You're not really a fit for your District. Reelection is going to be difficult unless we learn why and adjust on issues that really matter for them."

For Steve Weissman, Bob Hill's re-election was a tougher challenge than he had faced with Burt Egstrom, but he had worked miracles in the past.

Burt was re-elected.

Steve had run a successful challenge of an incumbent Republican Senator and established a way for election of his successor. He managed the campaigns for two Senate candidates by never permitting them to be seen in public!

Bob Hill's election was not a piece of cake and required a "remake" of Bob's public image.

A good marriage, Steve thought, would do much to earn the public's approval.

14.

A Marriage Made in Heaven

"Convinced" is too weak a word to describe Bob Hill's conviction, based on his experience at Betty Ford, that marriage to Apollonia was literally "made in heaven" and thought of the prospect as "a miracle."

But he had yet to take her to dinner. Then what?

Should he bring up his experience with the lady in the blue ball gown?

Bob rejected that idea. He didn't want her to think on their first date that he was, as Bob said to himself, "fucking nuts."

That he had been to a clinic for treatment of alcoholism was bad enough.

After all, she knew that Mary was killed when a car crashed into his vehicle when he was driving under the influence.

He had to address this relationship on the basis of "man meets woman," not "alcoholic meets a woman in his room at Betty Ford."

Besides, his mystic experience could be interpreted differently. After all, why a blue ball gown? Why did he buy a useless figurine from David Katz at the Coda gallery?

Wasn't this just an hallucination?

Any objective observer, especially a medical professional, would look for other explanations than the one that Bob Hill dragged up from a course he took at Harvard twenty-five years ago.

Yet, that experience was real and troubled Bob as he went into Landini's to meet "the woman of his dreams."

Dr. McCarthy's office called to say that she was late and would go directly to Landini's. And there she was when he arrived, dressed in an ivory muslin dress. Even Bob knew this was above the normal class of attire for dinner. But, Apollonia must have wanted Bob to know that she was "interested."

The plunging neckline of that dress was so alluring that during dinner Bob struggled to focus on Apollonia's face.

But what a face!

Her Greek ancestry from her mother mixed with her Irish genes inherited from her father created a "look" more common in marble statues that Bob had seen in the National Gallery and Boston's Museum of Fine Arts. That most were nude distracted his focus on Apollonia's face as she engaged him in conversation.

Her full lips, prominent nose, and ample breasts were distinctly Greek, but her curly auburn hair and light skin flecked with tiny freckles were as Irish as the air in County Cork.

Bob loved the pasta Pomodoro at Landini's, but this evening he could have eaten "Quaker's Oats" and enjoyed his dinner.

Apollonia shifted in her seat in a way so alluring that Bob lost focus and stared at those wonderful breasts covered so slightly by ivory muslin.

This evening could be a bust if he didn't get control of himself. So, down deep from his Pennsylvania past he asked, "Were there many Italians in Braddock when you were growing up?"

15.

Sen. and Mrs. Bob Hill

As Bob put it to Apollonia on their second date, "I don't believe in shitting around. Will you marry me?"

That began a round of planning the announcement and discussions about where.

Steve Weissman strongly suggested that the wedding take place in Pittsburgh at St. Paul's Cathedral in Oakland near the University of Pittsburgh. His official address was the Pittsburgh apartment of his Chief of Staff, and Apollonia had purchased a lovely home on Bayard Street within walking distance of St. Paul's, Pitt's Cathedral of Learning, the Carnegie Museum and Library, and Schenley Park.

Steve observed that Bayard Street was in the City of Pittsburgh that had been in control by Democrats longer than Finland had been subservient to the Soviet Union after it had lost its fight when Stalin's Red Army invaded in November 1939. The Finn's fought valiantly, killing 300,000 of Stalin's Red Army troops, but history, geography, and World War II decided that the Finns would submit to greater force.

Bob Hill often asked himself how the voters in Pittsburgh could submit to the Democrats longer than the Finn's existed in a subservient condition to the USSR.

After the wedding and re-election to the U.S. Senate, he would soon find out.

Apollonia would have preferred a wedding at St. Paul's Cathedral because it had been a part of her life since she attended Pitt. But. Sen. Hill said that his favorite priest, Fr. Peter Ford, at St. Augustine Church in Palm Desert, California, offered to marry them in a quiet ceremony. He made that observation in a way that Apollonia knew that was what Bob wanted.

It was October, and the weather in Pittsburgh wasn't as nice as Palm Desert, so Apollonia cleared her schedule at the Clinic, and she and Bob flew from BWI directly into Palm Springs where they checked into the Ritz Carlton at Rancho Mirage. The hotel was gorgeous, overlooking the Coachella Valley from a cliff top from which, at night, the lights of Palm Springs seemed to dance in unison.

To say it was romantic was an understatement, but

little did she expect the surprise she would experience upon meeting Fr. Peter Ford.

The short drive from the Ritz to St. Augustine Church took Bob through a route he remembered from his trip to Betty Ford with Chris Murphy. This time he made a note to arrange to dine at the Daily Grill on El Paseo in Palm Desert. That would be a good place to have dinner after the wedding ceremony.

The Daily Grill was a tossup with the Edge Steak-house at the Ritz-Carlton that features steaks, aged in-house for 21 to 65 days. Aged, prime beef was some-thing he enjoyed as a Congressman when he and Mary would drive to Baltimore's Mt. Washington where a lively piano bar and restaurant featured aged steaks. A visitor could view them aging in a special room and look forward to a good meal with music.

Fr. Peter Ford was delighted to see Sen. Hill again and to meet his bride.

"So," he said, "you're the lady in the blue ball gown." Sen. Hill's jaw dropped, and Fr. Ford realized that he had stepped into "deep doo doo."

"I'm sorry," Apollonia said, "what gal in what blue ball gown?"

16.

Fr. Peter Ford

As Fr. Ford ushered his guests into his study he whispered to Bob, "You didn't tell her?" Bob just shook his head.

"Well, I'm delighted to meet you, Apollonia. Bob has told me a lot about you, and Bob and I became good friends when he was at Betty Ford."

"I'm quite limited by rules of the confessional, but from my long experience as an Anglican priest, bartender and now Catholic priest, I am delighted that you've found a mate who lives up to your high standards. I visit Betty Ford weekly to say Mass and to talk to patients seeking advice and to administer the Sacrament of Penance. Bob, do you want to take it from there?"

"Honey," Bob said using a word he never said to Apollonia, "when I sought out Fr. Ford for advice, I was experiencing a problem. You see, at night I would be awakened by a figurine of a beautiful woman in a blue ball gown who miraculously came to life and would dance with me. That woman was you."

Blood rushed to Apollonia's head, and she felt weak. If she had fainted and fallen to the floor, her head would have rested on a book lying on the floor of Fr. Ford's study. The book was one that Fr. Ford had been reading the night before, a 462-page collection of G. K. Chesterton's three books, "Heretics," "Orthodoxy" and "The Everlasting Man."

"I'm sorry, but I don't understand."

Bob felt that unease that he had experienced the moment he revealed to Fr. Ford his "problem."

"Honey," when I was at Betty Ford I experienced your presence, felt your touch, and actually danced with you."

A pause.

"I know that sounds crazy, and that was why I was afraid to mention it. I explained it to myself as some-thing "mystic" and that it signified God's forgiveness of my sins and that I should have hope for the future. I didn't know that you were a real person, but you are and our love for one another is based on His love for us and all mankind."

Hearing that, Apollonia began to sob.

The wedding that followed the next day was witnessed by one of the older parishioners who had come to deliver a pound cake for Fr. Ford. Learning of the wedding, she enthusiastically agreed to attend as witness. And that was that. No flower arrangements. Just a wedding license and Fr. Ford.

17.

Walker's Planning

Charles Eisen had done a good job. His "Problem Detection" polling revealed that voters were exhausted by the 45th President of the United States. They literally wanted peace from "Twitter" messages, harangues against illegal immigrants, and the many nearly hot wars generated by the President's erratic rants.

The price of gas had risen to $8.00 a gallon and the federal deficit had reached historic levels. More important to Republican voters was the growth of the deficit relative to GDP. By 2019, the federal deficit had reached 4.6% of GDP. Most understood that wars increased deficit spending, and that contributed to the war weariness that engulfed the nation after the war with Iraq.

Retirees, Democrat and Republican, were sensitive to possible decreases in Social Security income, and young "Millennials" were aware that withholding taken from their pay would not translate into retirement benefits from Social Security thirty years later in 2054. Even by 2020, Social Security and Medicare benefits constituted more than 50% of federal spending.

Voter concern had not led to voter resolve to address the deficit "problem," so Charles Eisen arranged for George Walker to express concern but offer no resolutions.

Entitlements in 2024 were expected to remain a "Third Rail" of electoral politics.

Eisen knew that planning for a Presidential election in 2024 was long-term planning, but Eisen knew he needed to watch developments long before they kicked you in the teeth.

18.

Let the Brawl Begin

Sen. Bob Hill did not dislike his Senate colleague, George Walker.

He hated him.

That feeling was mutual and Sen. Walker was not saddened by his colleague's accident and DUI conviction.

Bob Hill, for his part, was not mean-spirited, but he believed that the Republican Party for too long had been controlled by "Big Government" politicians. Bob Taft, Barry Goldwater, and Ronald Reagan were his heroes, and he had nothing but contempt for politicians that he felt were representatives of Corporate America, whose loyalty gave the Party a bad name by deficit spending, imperial wars, and Wilsonian ideas of America's "democratic" mission.

Sen. George Walker symbolized everything that Bob despised and, as both Bob Hill and George Walker eyed the 2024 GOP presidential nomination, they both knew that they were in for a brawl of a lifetime.

Bob Hill, like most Republican politicians, was surprised that the 45th President literally stole his Party's nomination from those who had given their lives to sustain it, and he had to admit there were a few policies of the President that he liked.

Pennsylvania has always had a vigorous manufacturing sector, and manufacturing was challenged by foreign competition. "Free Trade" policies were given blame for the decline in manufacturing, but the mindset of career corporate executives was also to blame.

After World War II, U.S. manufacturers did not produce automobiles in Japan, and that failure was soon followed by the entry of Japanese autos into the American market. "Too damn fat and comfortable in Detroit," Bob said to himself.

And as he saw Pennsylvania's Steel producers lag behind foreign producers who quickly adopted new technologies that outstripped Pennsylvania steel companies, he became angrier. "Too fucking fat and comfortable," he said to startled members of his staff.

Pennsylvania workers in steel and coal were hurt by bad management and by the failure of their public schools. Many were Democrats who voted for the 45th

President because he called for protective tariffs. All "honorable" Republicans were for "Free Trade" and had clean fingernails because they never mined coal or worked in a mill.

Bob's relatives were mill hands and a cousin in West Virginia had worked in the mines. From them he understood that the American worker deserved more than to be displaced by foreign competition.

"Damn it," Bob Hill said, "America invented competition!"

Bob was also sympathetic to the 45th President's desire to block a stream of Syrians fleeing the collapse of civil society in Syria. He understood the desire of Brexit leaders to escape immigration of immigrants from other Muslim countries. And he commented caustically about Barack Obama's appeal to the EU to admit Turkey as a member.

"What the fuck is that all about?" he asked himself.

Though Bob was from Eastern Pennsylvania, he knew that many outside of Pittsburgh and Philadelphia were very conservative and lived in towns that he visited as he drove East from Allentown or Scranton to Western Pennsylvania. Towns like Wilkes-Barre, Bloomsburg, Reading, Chambersburg, Altoona, Johnstown and Indiana were so far apart from Democrat

Party politics of Philadelphia or Pittsburgh that James Carville thought they were similar to voters living in towns in Alabama.

The 45th President's complaint about voter fraud also rang true to Bob Hill who despised Joe Kenney, Mayor of Philadelphia, elected in 2015 with 85.4% of the general election vote. "That," said Bob, "is mathematically impossible unless you rigged the vote."

"Nobody carries 85% of the vote in any election," said Bob, "unless the winner steals the vote or is a Communist in Russia or a Nazi in Hitler's Germany."

He also thought the 45th President was dead right in criticizing former British Prime Minister Theresa May for dilly-dallying on Brexit and the three words he had to say about Germany's Angela Merkel who flooded Germany with a million Syrian émigrés were "She's fucking nuts."

Bob Hill wasn't a populist, nor did he buy into Steve Bannon's nationalism, but he watched Bannon closely as Bannon sold his form of nationalism, first to the 45th President and then to willing leaders in Hungary, Poland, and other former Soviet satellites.

Bob Hill was a "realist" about the national interest that turned him against the ideology of "Internationalism" that ignored the value of sovereignty and the national interest in favor of international law and international organizations. Bob hated the United Nations and approved moving that assembly from New York to Belgium. "Let them fuck one another and not us," he told Steve Weissman.

His assessment of Steve Weisman was heightened when he learned that once Weisman was so angered by parking tickets stacked on the inside console of a car with diplomatic plates parked outside the offices of one of his clients that he pissed into the car's open window.

Steve Weissman, like Bannon, had a vigorous business in Eastern Europe where he brought successful polling survey techniques to nationalist politicians in Prague, Hungary, Poland, and Croatia.

More important was Bob Hill's interest in key states in Presidential elections: Wisconsin, Pennsylvania, Michigan, and Florida. He knew something about each but made it a point to learn more. In Pennsylvania, his home state, he immersed himself in the history, personalities, and ethnic identities of Pennsylvanians in the central, Western, and northwest portions of the State.

In Michigan, he had good friends in Western Michigan and understood their pride in being "West Michiganders." He thought he could find support in south Florida and went out of his way to identify with the interests of Hispanics and younger voters of Cuban descent. He was aware that Cuba was still a Leftist center, but he went fishing in Cuba just to make a point.

He didn't think we should send troops to Central America, but these failed states needed to be knocked around a bit and the drug business marginalized. He favored spraying fields of poppy with insecticide and training and equipping pro-Western military in Mexico, Nicaragua, Guatemala, and Honduras to fight the drug gangs.

Nicaragua's Daniel Ortega was seventy-four, and control of Nicaragua would pass to younger men. "We need to know them," said Bob, and planned a fact-finding mission about education as soon as that could pass muster with State, the White House, and the Sandinista regime.

19.

Sen. George O Walker (R-OH)

George O Walker was planning his campaign to become the 46th President of the United States by running in opposition to everything that the two-term 45th President of the United States stood for. But, first, he had to win re-election to the Senate.

Though the 45th President and he were raised not more than 500 miles apart, they might just as well have come from another country. He was from the mid-West and the 45th President was from a borough of New York City.

Each came from different ends of the political spectrum, the one a New Deal Democrat turned Republican and Walker, an Ohio Republican, who focused on his constituents. The one born into wealth, the other still trying to make his fortune. Walker didn't know if the 45th President would support him, his Democrat opponent, or a Republican primary opponent, and, frankly, didn't give a damn.

Walker had been radicalized in college and, though he kept his views close to his chest, he was committed to a policy of the Big Government Republicanism of former President George W. Bush.

In response to what the 45th President of the United States believed was central to American life and culture, Sen. Walker intended to present himself as an agent for change.

Walker attended church, sent his kids to a religious school, and never cheated on his wife. The 45th President had an active libido, never went to church, and had been married three times. In the vernacular of the "street," the 45th President was a "rounder."

Walker knew what he wanted to accomplish while the President he wanted to succeed wanted to know what his electoral "base" wanted and adopted those policies.

The 45th President was tall, good-looking and throughout life got by on "looks" and inherited wealth.

Walker disdained alcohol and ate his way through life. Like William Howard Taft, who at 5' 11 1/2" weighed three hundred and fifty pounds, Senator Walker was also obese, weighing in at two hundred and fifty pounds, but was only 5' 4".

Raised in Ohio, he had a knack for transcending the differences of factions of his own Party. Everyone liked George, and George Walker liked those who liked him.

Ohio is a mid-Western state between the East Coast of the United States and the far West. Growing up in Ohio, George Walker understood that everything east of the Ohio river was "East Coast," so Sen. Bob Hill's Pennsylvania was lumped in his mind with New York, Massachusetts, and Vermont—not the mid-West that he knew and loved.

Ohio politicians lacked hard edges that are visible in the indignation of Tea Party conservatives when they hear the words "Big Government." After all, Big Government, George Walker said to himself, had been beneficial to Ohio from a series of Ohioans from William Howard Taft to Bob Taft to John Kasich to George O Walker.

George Walker didn't think much about Gov. John Bricker of Ohio who served in the U.S. Senate from 1939-1945 and introduced the "Bricker Amendment." That Amendment to the Constitution of the United States limited the President from entering into executive agreements with foreign governments and ensured that treaties in conflict with the Constitution would require Congressional enabling legislation.

Nor did Senator Walker think much of Senator Bob Taft's stand against Big Labor and his opposition to the Nuremberg Tribunals.

Sen. Taft argued that making new laws to apply to past actions was a form of *ex post facto* legislation that is prohibited by the Constitution of the United States.

Those were different times, with more contentious issues than ones today, and Bob Taft's issues of the 1940s had no value for success in elective politics eighty years later.

Sen. Walker's avoidance of issues made him seem homey and "mid-West." His middle initial "O" expressed the amazement of his father who said "Oh" with emphasis when he learned that his wife had given birth to a son. So, Sen. George "O" Walker like President Harry "S" Truman had no middle name.

There were other things about George Walker that annoyed the hell out of Sen. Bob Hill. For one thing, Sen. Walker had a fat, smart, calculating pollster whose one successful run for office was a campaign for president of his senior class in high school.

Charles Eisen was representative of a new class of political consultants who only believe in getting elected and holding and using power. The skills of consultants like Eisen were legendary and backed by a system of reward and punishment.

Though Eisen's clients were Republicans, he was rooted in a new morality that hated tradition and its defenders.

Bob Hill learned that the hard way when Sen. Walker sponsored an expansion of government programs in education, and Sen. Hill organized a group of Senators to vote against it. Bob Hill's colleague, Senator Bud Omohundro, also from Ohio, took him aside and warned him that he can't do that to George.

"He will never forget and he will attempt to punish you and do everything possible to assure that he beats you good."

"Oh come on, Bud," Sen. Hill replied, "my consti-tuents in Pennsylvania know me and would not permit a Senator from fucking Ohio, of all places, to injure me."

"Whatever you say, Bob, but, believe me; Charles Eisen is a hater and will move very quickly to punish you if you oppose Bob Walker on this education issue."

"My constituents love me, and I love them, " Bob Hill replied. "I have to vote against Walker's shit ass proposal. They'll understand."

Sen. Hill had made "education" his own issue and curried favor with Home School and Charter School advocates by advocating for school "Choice."

What he knew about what went on in those Charter School classrooms was little to nothing, but it was the principle of the thing and by advocating freedom from a public school monopoly Sen. Hill earned the loyalty of serious people of both parties.

Like Charles Eisen, Sen. George O Walker also loved to hate, which was another reason that he annoyed Senator Bob Hill. Bob considered himself a lover, not a hater, and often said "Life is too short to be wasted on hate."

George O Walker was very different.

Though a Methodist by virtue of his mother's piety, he didn't know much about Methodism. His religion was his political career.

Nothing much stood in his way as he moved up the political ladder. Serving first as a campaign worker while in college, he ran for the Ohio state Senate as soon as he graduated. By the time he ran, he had been active in Cleveland politics for four years and knew everyone. He decided where to run, moved into that district, and was elected.

Elective office was new to him, but he was not surprised by the way the Party controlled legislation. "To get along, go along" was the standard that became his way of looking at things, so he moved quickly and became leader of the younger members of the state Senate.

The one thing George O Walker wouldn't do was take a bribe. Once as he was walking to the office of one of his colleagues in the Ohio State Senate, George Walker decided to walk down the back stairs, rather than take the elevator two floors down from his office. On the way down, a man he met on the landing asked him to vote for a measure he opposed and offered him $5,000. Sen. Walker shouted, "That's a bribe!" and went back to his office.

Back in his office he quickly sized up what had happened and made an important decision. He would get the hell out of the Ohio state legislature and run for Congress.

Deciding to run, and doing it, were two different calculations. The two Congressmen in Districts near where he lived were senior, older men, and part of the Party's Establishment. Fortunately for George, both died within six months of each other, and George made his move.

As a new member of the U.S. House of Representatives, he enjoyed the opportunity that the House had a Republican majority for the first time since 1952—

thanks to Newt Gingrich and his "Contract with America."

Those were heady times since George O Walker was a post-World War II baby, and 1994 was the first sign of political success for persons who had not fought in World War II.

The World War II generation had dominated American politics because they lived longer than their parents but had fewer children. Their children, therefore, represented a much smaller portion of the American population, and the oldsters weren't willing to give an inch to the younger generation. They all spoke a good game about the younger generation but in reality they didn't want them competing against them, nor did they give them a shot at working for them.

Young conservative Republicans quickly realized that Ronald Reagan's Administration was salted with World War II generation appointees, and the young conservatives who made his election possible were shunted aside.

Reagan's was an "old man's" Administration, George Walker concluded, and only the respect for authority of the post-World War II generation kept them from rebelling against Reagan.

Ronald Reagan was an old man and couldn't understand those who were forty years younger.

Though that was then, and by 2019 Walker was 70, that generational bias, or revolt of youth, spurred George O Walker to push aside the old men who stood in his way as he moved up the ladder, but he also liked pushing them out.

He liked hunting because of a love of the kill, and he loved politics because he loved how he felt when he destroyed those in his way.

That explained why Americans living in 2020 who were post-World War II generation 'babies' liked George Walker and voted for his election to the United States Senate from Ohio after serving only one term in the U.S. House of Representatives.

As far as Bob Hill was concerned, George Walker was a typical Ohio politician, too proud of his down-home origins and fatter than some blimps.

Bob made a note to inquire about the cost of a blimp that looked like Walker.

20.

The Race is On

Charles Eisen was the genius behind the successful election of George Walker to the U.S. Senate. Eisen was loathed in part because his polls were usually right and because he was fat, a slovenly dresser who preferred tennis shoes, and was boastful.

Charles Eisen was not only the genius behind the successful election of George Walker to the U.S. Senate in 2014 but was also preparing his 2020 campaign for re-election to the Senate while planning a run for the White House in 2024.

What made Eisen good was his complete absorption in political history, tactics, and technology. He got his start working for a campaign pollster who taught him how to design survey questions and analyze the results.

Watching Eisen explain polling surveys was a sight to behold. He kept the surveys in a three-ring binder and brought them to his client's office where he showed what their strengths were and what weaknesses needed to be remedied. When the meeting ended, he took his surveys with him.

Though Eisen was a great strategist, he wasn't a principled conservative, nor did he have even what passes for "Republican" values, so if a client's polling indicated that he needed to appeal to voters who disagreed with a client's views or principles, he didn't hesitate to tell him to change. In other words, Charles Eisen wasn't rooted philosophically. At heart, he was a political Liberal.

Eisen's father worked as an administrator in the Ohio Mutual Insurance company his entire career. Though not wealthy, he took care of his family and made it possible for Charles to attend Gilmour Academy, a good private school in Gates Mill, Ohio. Gilmour was founded by Holy Cross priests from Notre Dame, and though Eisen's father was a Presbyterian, he thought it best to enroll Charles in a school that had rules, a work ethic and charitable inclinations. Gilmour also had a good golf team, and Charles mastered golf well enough to make the team and hold his own in local tournaments.

Gilmour was a small enough school that a student

wouldn't fall through the cracks and large enough to give students a way to compare their skills and personalities with the skills and talents of a variety of other students. Charles did well in Math and upon graduation from Gilmour he was admitted to Miami University of Ohio.

At Miami, Eisen chose Business Administration as his major and encountered a professor who had retired from a major New York advertising firm.

Raymond Osborn was a son of Alex Osborn, one of the founders of BBDO.

Osborn the younger was a Chemistry major at Harvard and went on to earn a Ph.D. in Mathematics from MIT. His first academic appointment was teaching Statistics at Carnegie Mellon, but when a position opened in the Research Division of BBDO, Ray Osborn joined his late father's firm in New York.

There he made a mark in survey research by designing what he called a "Problem Detection" survey that identified what problems people had and what could be done to solve them.

That craftsmanship made him a star at BBDO and helped BBDO's clients like Chrysler, Wrigley, Burger King and many others. For Wrigley, Osborn's surveys enabled "Big Red" chewing gum to outsell its competitor, Dentyne. Osborn's surveys led to the development of Burger King's "Whopper," and he was so good that Lee Iacocca threatened to pull the Chrysler account if Osborn Left BBDO to accept an offer to work in the Reagan White House.

Finding out what problems people had, and fashioning ways to solve those problems, intrigued Charles Eisner. He mastered his teacher's Problem Detection survey research method and adapted it to consulting work for Republican campaigns.

His survey work caught the eye of young George Walker when he decided to run for a Congressional seat. Eisner's "smarts" and surveys gave Walker the edge he needed to win that first campaign for federal office, and they became inseparable.

There is a difference between knowing what people want and offering public policies that are consistent with a philosophy of limited government. In the case of Charles Eisen, his knowledge of what problems people wanted solved led him to develop policies that forced their problems into the forefront and the resolution of those policies into the background. Eisen became an expert in the politics of hate.

There was plenty of room for Eisen to operate because Ohio never had a conservative movement, and politics was largely a contest between those who flattered voters the most.

As a result, when manufacturing in Ohio took a hit in 2007, by then Governor of Ohio, Walker reached into the public purse to create a "jobs" program. No other politician active at the time—except Bob Hill—competed with Walker by suggesting that cuts in taxes and state regulations were the better way to go than "spending."

But, then, Walker had held elective office since graduating from university. He didn't pay attention to entrepreneurs except when asking successful ones for political donations. The economic conditions that enable entrepreneurs to excel was a "vision thing" best left to dreamers. When he decided he would run to become the 46th President of the United States in 2024, Walker didn't anticipate that Sen. Bob Hill was also interested in moving from the Senate to the White House.

Early on, Walker, a keen observer of other politicians, wrote off Bob Hill as a drunk.

21.

Re-Election

Steve Weissman directed his staff to create a press release that stated that Sen. Bob Hill had married a physician originally from Pittsburgh, Dr. Apollonia McCarthy, and the couple would reside in Pittsburgh. He ordered that be done by staff since he was never a "writer." Math whiz, yes. Intuitive genius who could see demographic patterns that for others were just "numbers," yes. But, creative writer?

After putting the "good news" wedding announcement in place, he could go about preparing for Bob's re-election.

Steve took nothing for granted and simultaneous with organizing a campaign he brought aboard a campaign fundraiser to build up the campaign's finances. Everyone called her "General" Furman because Jen was a control freak fixed on raising big donations with words.

Everything had a place, and if something wasn't in its place, she made George Patton sound like Mother Teresa. Nobody much minded because she was a natural beauty with blue eyes, blonde hair, and skin as white as her ample breasts—plus she was good at her craft. And when words failed, she sometimes put body English into her appeal. It was rumored that she raised $5 million to start a PAC over a weekend on the yacht of a major media czar.

Steve figured he needed about $5 million for the primary and another $20 million for the General. Most registered voters receive letters requesting donations, and Jen was one of those writers who had perfected these types of letters.

There are letters from the candidate, his wife, and sometimes his mother. They are usually long and end with an appeal accompanied by a form to indicate how much you're donating and a return envelope. Many include a return stamp and some are sent in 6 x 9 envelopes to distinguish them from more common types of appeals.

More than 100,000 donations of $100 or less were raised by the Goldwater campaign, and those 100,000 donors launched the direct mail fundraising business.

One very astute conservative visited the government office after the 1964 election where names and addresses of donors were filed and copied their names and addresses—by hand!

Jen put a great deal of effort into that first fund-raising letter sent to medical doctors in Pennsylvania and a second one was sent to Steve's Primary voters list and signed by Dr. Apollonia Hill!

The letter, printed on expensive paper with a bluish tint, began with three sentences:

Dear Colleague,

You and I know how hard it is to balance our professional duties and build a loving family. It took me a number of years to realize that I could be a better doctor if I found a supporting man who understood the challenges we face.

I'm writing to let you know that I found that person."

With the letter, Jen enclosed a photo of a beaming Apollonia and Senator Bob Hill.

Sen. Charles Walker was surprised by news of Bob

Hill's marriage and especially surprised that Bob was running for re-election. Because Sen. Walker had written Bob Hill off as a drunk, he had been relieved that he wouldn't have to run against him for President. After re-election to the Senate, that was Charles Eisen and Sen. Walker's sole priority, and he quickly forgot about his Senate colleague.

Bob Hill had not forgotten Charles Walker and was more than concerned that another "Big Government" Republican might become President of the United States. But Steve Weissman's and Sen. Hill's sole priority was re-election to the United States Senate in 2020.

Steve Weissman's surveys revealed that voters were aware that Bob was involved in a fatal accident in which he was cited for DUI.

A DUI will kill any political career, but DUI leading to the death of your wife?

Steve knew that was something that killed Bob Hill's chances for re-election and removing that stain from his candidate's reputation became Steve's obsesssion.

It was a long shot, but because he came from Brooklyn, he decided to contact some friends who had gone to school with him at CUNY. Steve and his friends agreed to meet at a steak house in the Williamsburg area of Brooklyn.

Bob asked his staff to make a note of this and focused on how he could attract some Democrats to break ranks and vote for Bob Hill.

He decided to do this the easy way by bribing two Union leaders to throw their Union's support to Bob, and two weeks before the election he provided African American pastors of AME churches in Philadelphia and Pittsburgh with wads of "walking around money."

Steve knew something about bribes. As a young Intern in the local Brooklyn GOP headquarters, he was asked to witness the giving of a bribe to a prominent leader of the Democrats. The chief of staff of the headquarters and he drove out to Long Island and upon coming to a vacant field, Steve noticed a man standing in the middle of the field. The staff person said "Wait here," reached behind his seat, pulled out a paper bag and walked toward the man in the field. Steve had witnessed the payment of a bribe and could vouch for it, if needed.

He knew little about African Methodist ministers, but he was a keen observer and knew from previous campaign events in Pittsburgh and Philadelphia that both cities had African American leaders who were ministers. He remembered one church, south of Pitts-

burgh's "Hill District" in an area called Bloomfield, and
drove there.

He found the church choir practicing for Sunday
service. The choir of six middle-age women and one
male were accompanied by a pianist, drummer, and
choir leader with castanets.

Steve listened while his eyes searched the small
chapel for the church's pastor. These small churches
were the places where some of the greatest female
vocalists were discovered before they encountered a
worldly life much more complicated than this small
Bloomfield church.

Steve didn't have to search far to find the church
pastor since Pastor Eugene jumped to the front of the
chapel and began to dance and sing a rap melody about
coming back to church.

A fit 35-year-old, in a well-fitting brown suit,
Pastor Eugene was clearly a spiritual force to be
reckoned with. Now Steve had to decide if Pastor
Eugene could become a political force for Bob Hill.

22.

"CUNY"

City University of New York, popularly referred to as "CUNY," was a godsend to the children of poor New York City immigrants. If they worked part time in their parent's food stand or rag carts, they could go to college and make something of themselves.

The names of CUNY graduates who became New York city "literati" could be counted in the hundreds. Many of them were the children of Jews who fled the Bolshevik revolution in Russia and later fled the Nazi's in World War II.

Growing up, they lived in a "melting pot," meeting people from places that Americans in the mid-West never knew existed, places like Ruthenia, Ukraine, Silesia, Trieste, or Serbia.

At CUNY, some of Steve's classmates were children of members of Mafia families. Their daughters, especially, were tough and dismissive of laws, due process, and the police. If you fucked one of them, Steve understood, you better make certain that she wanted it. And if she became pregnant, you had to marry her—or else!

23.

Down to Business

A campaign for election of an incumbent United States Senator in any state, but especially Pennsylvania, had to avoid a primary challenger and hold constant meetings with voters.

"Press the flesh" was not a metaphor, and woe to the successful politician who liked DC better than his home District and thought he could cruise to re-election.

There is always someone in the wings who thinks he can beat an incumbent, and the trick to winning is to avoid a Primary contest.

There are two kinds of voters: "Primary" voters and those who show up, not often, but sometimes, to vote in General Elections.

More would vote in a Presidential election year, and that made the re-election of Bob Hill a "wild card."

President 45 was running for re-election in 2020 as

were Bob Hill and George Walker.

A Primary voter is someone who takes politics seriously and always votes in Primary Elections, Fortunately, there are lists of Primary election voters, and Steve had secured and cleansed a list of primary voters of the deceased and those whose addresses had changed and set up a chain of letters and post cards that each would receive.

He carefully conducted surveys by phone and had a pretty good sense of where they stood on issues and what and how they viewed Bob Hill.

The first phone surveys revealed that more needed to be said about Dr. Apollonia McCarthy and her marriage to Bob Hill.

Planning of the first campaign events were designed to bring voters to understand more about Apollonia and that she was a medical Doctor. Their approval of Apollonia would rub off on his candidate.

On Sundays or Saturday nights, Bob and Apollonia would walk to St. Paul's Cathedral and be seen on that weekly walk. After mass, they would attend either a Pittsburgh Pirates or Steelers' game, and Steve made sure they were seen at these events.

In the old days, Pittsburgh's Dick Scaife, heir to a Mellon fortune, would assure that the county and state

GOP had plenty of funding.

Now it was necessary to attract donations from a variety of sources.

Pittsburgh was a major medical center, and requests for donations were sent to medical professionals under Apollonia's signature.

Bob's service on two important Senate committees were another source of donations, and Steve created several PACs that could accept unlimited donations.

That was the easy part. The major obstacle to Bob Hill's re-election was that damn fatal accident.

24.

A Good Steak

Will Palambretta was a Mafia soldier who had been in some of Steve Weisman's classes at CUNY and spent a four-year sentence at Leavenworth. It was a minor slight, but Steve reacted violently to being called "Bacciagaloop."

Steve visited Will for two reasons: to renew their brief friendship that they shared at CUNY and to ask him to "check something out."

Steve was intrigued that after the fatal accident in which Mary Hill was killed, the driver of the other car had disappeared. If anyone could find him, Will Palambretta could.

Will contacted three members of his Mafia family, his cousin, Joe "the razor" Aiello, Louie "steel bar" Camp and Phil "grease gun" Amaretto. All of them had attended Bishop Loughlin Memorial High School about two miles from where they met for dinner.

Peter Luger's steak house in the Williamsburg section of Brooklyn was famous for aged steaks as big as the plates on which they were served. A meal at Luger's steak house is a celebration, and those who were "regulars" had ties to the neighborhood.

In the 80s, that section of Brooklyn was becoming 'hip," with trendy bars and clubs and the beginnings of an art colony. The ethnic mix hadn't changed much since the 1960's when Hasidic Jews lived in hatred of African Americans from "Bedford Sty" and a sizeable Irish and Italian population.

Twenty years earlier, intermarriage between Irish and Italians was not encouraged, but coming to be accepted. "Razor" and "Grease" had Irish mothers. Steel Bar's father was a "soldier" in the Mob. All their fathers took care of their boys by giving them a good high school education at Bishop Loughlin.

Will went on to CUNY where he studied Business Administration. Razor and Greese enlisted in the Army where they spent time in Germany near the Fulda Gap. Steel Bar got a job at the Brooklyn Navy Yard and was recruited to join the Mob. They were all good boys who enjoyed growing up in Brooklyn, respected the elderly, and took care of their "bros."

They met for dinner at Peter Lugars.

25.

Blood Red Moon over Miami

"Here's the deal," said Will. "You remember Steve Weissman? He's working for a candidate for the Senate, Bob Hill, who got into deep shit when a car he was driving was involved in an accident. His wife was killed, and his career was shit. The accident was a media circus, and since Hill is a Republican Senator, he was immediately tried, convicted, and sentenced by the national media. Nobody paid attention to the driver of the car that hit the Senator's car.

"This fella," said Will pulling a photo from his inside coast pocket, "has disappeared."

"We tried to look him up, but he quit his job as a cook at a Capitol Hill eatery, moved from his DC apartment, and was last believed to be living in Miami.

Find him, and find out why he was driving down that street just in time to hit the Senator's car."

Sure enough, the other driver had served a brief

time at Leavenworth. He admitted that he had been paid to target Bob Hill, waited for him to leave the Mayflower, and intentionally ran into his car intending just to send Sen. Hill a message.

Who paid him? "Charles Eisen," a now-bloody informant said.

Steve struggled to find his cell phone and called Bob Hill and shouted "Your accident was a hit!"

"You were targeted by someone Charles Eisen paid to send you a message not to fuck with George Walker."

26.

How Clear is the Air

Bob Hill hadn't realized fully how wracked with guilt he was. After all, he had been convicted in Court for drunk driving and involuntary manslaughter. For two very long years, he lived with loss of his wife and all that he had worked for in American politics.

One day, he was a washed up "pol," and the next he was exonerated from responsibility in the death of his wife.

The miracle of a statue gave him the unquestioned love of Apollonia and renewal of his hope that he might serve his country.

The air in Pittsburgh had been cleaned up since the mid-1950s though the decline of Big Steel left cities like Pittsburgh, Allentown, Philadelphia, Erie, and all the small towns in-between facing a stark reality: physical labor was insufficient, knowledge was needed; Pennsylvania's public education was woefully inadequate in preparing Pennsylvanians for productive careers, local taxes were too high, and stifled entrepreneurs who wanted to stay in Pennsylvania and start new businesses and the bedrock of orthodox religions was weakened by what could only be called a "loss of faith."

Pennsylvania's private colleges and universities were competent, but they too were afflicted by ideologies that challenged traditional disciplines especially in the Arts and Humanities.

With every sign that Bob Hill was living in an era of political and cultural decline, on a personal level Bob Hill felt great!

27.

Pennsylvania Up-Close

If you want to see a state, region, or an entire country warts and all, run for political office.

And that's what Bob Hill planned to do as he sought re-election to the U.S. Senate. Exoneration for the death of Mary Hill gave him an immediate boost and cleared the decks of those who were planning to replace him. And anyone planning a primary challenge had to think twice or three times.

Primary races are expensive, and Steve Weissman had put into place a formidable fundraising system that waited only for that exoneration that Weissman sensed was sure to come.

Without a primary challenge, Steve figured he needed twenty million dollars to wage a campaign for re-election of a sitting U.S. Senator, and the General Election required not less than twenty million. Reaching those goals were in the hands of Jen Furman and on the trail to eating away large numbers of African American voters Weissman went back to visit Pastor Eugene at the AME Church in Bloomfield.

Bloomfield used to be called "babushka" territory with row after row of townhomes where old women wearing babushkas lived. Most were from Eastern Europe and spoke accented American English. Their children had moved to the suburbs or out of state where better economic opportunity could be found. Miami and Tucson were preferred because the weather was warm and the air clear. Many who moved from Pittsburgh to Arizona felt their nasal passages cleared of congestion, and they could smell the scent of flowers for the first time in their lives.

Grandma would have to travel on jet airplanes—for the first time—to visit her grandkids. And she saw her children in Bloomfield only when funerals for members of the family demanded their presence.

Babushka ladies and African Americans voted Democrat, and what had been comfortable Republican margins in the suburbs had eroded by the second year of President 45's second term.

Suburbs of Philadelphia like Bryn Maw and Fox Chapel in Pittsburgh where wealthy families lived comfortable lives moved into the Democrat column.

In-between Philly and Pittsburgh—what John Carville called "Alabama"—small towns were economic disasters.

A drive from Pittsburgh to Erie would find vacant strip malls and closed gas stations until you arrived at Grove City where a major center of Outlets attracted overnight shoppers.

Allentown on the Eastern part of Pennsylvania, north of Philadelphia, was thriving from Pennsylvanians who commuted to work in New York City or were employed in the many colleges concentrated nearby.

If the cost of college tuition increased, or a recession broke the back of the strong economy much touted as the doing of President 45, unemployment would swell.

Bob Hill's task was to thread the needle between three extremes: traditional Democrat voters, a Republican President seeking re-election and Republicans challenged by President 45's erratic tweets and his arousal of what the media was calling "tribal" divisions in civil society.

Critical to supporting a campaign for re-election were ensuring the President's support, attracting African American pastors to his candidacy, engaging working class white voters, consolidating Republican support in the suburbs, and assuring that Republican primary voters voted in the General Election.

Sen. Hill had to confirm President 45s support, and he did that by appearing on Fox News and expressing his admiration of policies that the President liked.

Pennsylvania's manufacturing sector was challenged by foreign competition. Bob Hill said that corporate executives failed to respond to competition. He pointed to delays in adapting new technologies in steel production and the failure to market American automobiles in Japan.

Bob made it a point of pride that some of his relatives were mill hands and said he had a plan to displace foreign competition on what he called a "tit for tat" basis. The Japanese were notorious in forcing changes in exported products thus making them more expensive.

"That will stop," he said.

Bob also said he opposed immigration of Muslims and pointed at the problem in major European cities where non-Muslims dared not go. He told his listeners about the time he was in Hamburg, Germany, and missed his stop on the subway. "I was lucky to get out of Hamburg alive," he said.

He also took time to show his understanding of changes in European politics by explaining why British nationalists wanted to get out from the open borders imposed on European Union member nations.

And when speaking to white working class voters, he criticized Barack Obama's appeal to the EU to admit Turkey as a member.

That worked, and President 45 invited Senator and Mrs. Hill to an intimate dinner at the White House.

Bob Hill was then introduced to Pastor Eugene at the Bloomfield AME Church that Steve Weismann scoped out.

Pastor Eugene displayed openness to the Senator's appeal for support, and Jen Furman arranged to meet the good Pastor for dinner at Station Square. In the ornate dining room that once was the Grand Concourse of a Pennsylvania railroad, Jen explained that she was the dispenser of "walking around" money and agreed to meet up again for dinner in late October. Before leaving, she asked if Pastor Eugene might hold a meeting for Senator Hill with other AME pastors and suggested that it would be great if his church choir would sing at the gathering—for a fee, of course.

Meetings with Republicans in Bryn Mawr were more difficult. Too many women were offended by

President 45, and it was hard to admit having dinner at the White House and express his anger at the President's behavior. In some ten meetings like that, Dr. Apollonia McCarthy did the talking.

And in Allentown where, by Bob Hill's count, some ten colleges enrolled more than 20,000 college students, Bob gave a major speech on the student loan problem.

"I have a plan to lower tuition cost," he said.

A campaign for the U.S. Senate is like a forced march during a war, and Bob worked out each morning, building strength in his arms and legs. He loved yoghurt and would keep some handy for "snacking." At the end of this ordeal, Bob had lost another ten pounds and looked even younger than he did after leaving Betty Ford.

28.

Mission Accomplished

The indictment of Charles Eisen for complicity in the assault on Senator Hill hit Ohio politics like a plane wreck. George Walker's relationship with Eisen was well-known, and some voters felt it curious, to say the least, that Sen. Walker knew nothing about it.

Contributions to Walker's re-election campaign dropped precipitously. Only Walker's long-time service in Ohio government kept him alive politically.

There was also the loyalty factor that was unique to Ohio politics. Two former Governors and Ohio's other Republican Senator gave their support to their "friend."

Exposure of Eisen's perfidy gave Steve Weissman the means he needed to reshape Sen. Hill's approval rating. The 2020 Pennsylvania Senate race was close, but Bob Hill was re-elected.

And, due to the loss of the services of Charles Eisen, Sen. Walker of Ohio almost lost his campaign for re-election.

About the Author

Richard J. Bishirjian is a scholar, businessman and education entrepreneur. *Coda* is his first attempt at writing fiction, though some things he has written in order to raise financing came very close to being fictive.

He earned a B.A. from the University of Pittsburgh, and a Ph.D. in Government and International Studies from the University of Notre Dame where he studied with Eric Voegelin and completed a Ph.D. dissertation under the direction of Gerhart Niemeyer.

He did advanced study with Michael Oakeshott at the London School of Economics and studied Sanskrit at the Southern Asia Institute, Columbia University, Latin at Loyola University-Chicago and classical Greek at Hunter College in New York.

Dr. Bishirjian taught at universities and colleges in Indiana, Texas and New York and was founding President of Yorktown University. He has written extensively on the role of philosophy in ameliorating the effects of relativism, the intellectual disease of

American culture.

Other books by the author:

- *A Public Philosophy Reader* (1978)

- *The Development of Political Theory: A Critical Analysis* (1978)

- *The Conservative Rebellion* (2015)

- *The Coming Death and Future Resurrection of American Higher Education* (2017)

- *Rise and Fall of the American Empire*, accepted for publication by Hamilton Books, 2020.

- *Conscience and Power: The Contest for Civilization in the West*, has been submitted for publication.